Dear ~~~~~ ~~~~

Thanks for your
enormous efforts
to make no a
home. You are
The Original
Franny for The
Franny Project
within The DMH.

Lisa
Fay

HOME

within the DMH

Fay

HOME

William E Burleson
Editor

Flexible Press

Minneapolis, Minnesota

2019

ISBN 978-1-7339763-2-9
Flexible Press
William E Burleson
Editor

About Flexible Press: Flexible Press is dedicated to supporting authors, communities, and mission-driven non-profits through story. Somewhere between some and all of the profits from Flexible Press titles are donated to relevant non-profits. Find out more at www.flexiblepub.com.

Associate editors

Stephen Wilbers

Megan Marsnik

Advisory committee

Ed Sheehy

Don Browne

Stephen Parker

Teresa Ortiz

Copy Editor: Vicki Adang,
Mark My Words Editorial Services, LLC

Cover photo: depositphotos.com

This book is dedicated to all those in
search of home, and to all those
who help make that search
just a little easier.

Thank you

Thank you to the stellar advisory committee and readers who did the heavy lifting. This has been a team effort from the start.

Thank you to all the wonderful authors—both those who are included herein and those who could not be—who let us read their amazing work.

And thank you, dear reader, for supporting these authors and supporting the cause of bringing an end to homelessness.

—*William E Burleson, editor*

IN SEARCH OF HOME

As you drive west out of the Twin Cities into farm country, the land flattens into the Great Plains. Views are horizon to horizon, and trees are scarce, other than in stands of trees usually well off the highway. These trees are often at the end of long dirt driveways with a house sometimes visible in the center. Living on the Plains means having an appreciation for planting trees as windbreaks in anticipation of the howling winds of January coming in from the Dakotas.

The distances between these stands of trees anchored by houses are quite regular. When the land was originally stolen from the Dakota, it was divided into squares and given away or sold for pennies to European settlers. The unit of transaction was a quarter section, a section being one mile by one mile. This pattern is most obvious from above, a checkerboard running across a wide swath of the country.

However, closer inspection reveals that not all of these stands of trees have driveways to them, or at least maintained ones. If you made your way up the unmaintained drive or across the fields to these islands of cottonwoods and oaks, you would likely find a wood-framed two-story house; but rather than well maintained and warm with cut grass and trimmed hedges, it would be decaying and overgrown, dark and dead. Rather than a home, it is more of a prairie ghost ship.

The story of these ghost houses is a common one: Immigrants built houses and broke fields in the tall grass prairie (no small task). They had families. They raised chickens. They baked pies and bought pianos from Sears. And oftentimes they quit. Maybe it happened in short order, selling their newly acquired land at a tidy profit, and maybe it happened later, in a forced auction. No matter the story, the farm was sold to their neighbors, and the people moved on, leaving ever larger farms and a small cluster of trees and a house in decay.

These houses, like the one on the cover of this book, exist all over farm country, a testament to immigrant optimism colliding with sometimes harsh reality. As a result, a home that was once warm and light, wallpapered and filled with piano music, is now a place for kids to get high until, eventually, the gray structure returns to the earth.

An apt metaphor for how sometimes home doesn't work out the way we want it to.

"Threshing" by Nancy Louise Cook tells the story of one such failed farm on the prairie, one of the stories of immigrants in search of a home in this anthology. But most stories in *Home* by or about the immigrant experience are more contemporary, such as a young woman has to navigate the realities of her parents being deported in "America," while "Lemonade on a Lakeside Bench" takes the other point of view, of an elderly man recognizing—and embracing—change. New Minnesotans also bring their stories. Minnesota's own celebrated Ahmed Yusuf offers us a tale of his home of origin in "A Slow Moving Night," as does Teresa Ortiz in "The Children's Mountain." In contrast, Wing Young Huie tells a different sort of immigrant story in "Where Are You Really From?" one where he is not in any way an immigrant but is seen as one, regardless.

Trying to build a new home for oneself in a new land is but one story of struggle. Sometimes home is something we once had and now long to regain. Quite the opposite of an immigrant, Grace Smith endures the horror of an Indian boarding school and travels thousands of miles before finally discovering home again in "I Am from Pitkas Point, Alaska." Sometimes it's a struggle to make a home, as when Heidi Arneson struggles to keep her home from ruin in "My Homework Ate Me." Sometimes it's a struggle to belong at all, as in David Jauss's "Firelight." And sometimes it's a struggle with outsiders who are trying to deny your right to your own home, as in Yvonne's "Ballad of the Arthur and Edith Lee House."

However, not all stories are about struggle. Many of the stories, memoirs, and poems in this anthology are about remembering the feeling of home, of belonging, of pies baking, despite the challenges that are thrown in front of us. In Mary Karlsson's "The Kitchen in the Cinderblock House," the constant is home. Sometimes home is not a building, but Minnesota itself, as in Crystal Gibbins's trip through the beauties that are Minnesota in "Driving North."

The twenty-eight authors who make up *Home* each offer the reader their own journey toward home, their own struggles and triumphs. But whatever the journey, the constant throughout is a human constant: We all want to belong, to have our place in the world not be conditional, violent, nor violating. We all want to feel warm, smell the pie, and play the piano. Although it doesn't always work out that way, and while it is seldom easy, we still keep looking, each of us on our own personal search for home.

HOME

Now, as I near the end of my days, I wonder how we come to call a place: home. Born there, perhaps. A job. Climate. Family roots, getting away from something, love. None of those have dictated my decisions in this regard. I was a trades-man, a laborer really, all my life, and could do a number of simple things passably well. Worked in several factories and on a number of construction projects. Spent a fair amount of time in the merchant marines. Helped on a few ranches, drove trucks, welded. A lifetime of doing this and that in this or that place.

One time, about twenty-five years ago, I was heading from one place to the next, driving from Seattle across the Great Plains to Omaha to work with a cousin who had recently started a painting business there. It was late fall. All the corn had been turned under; the fields were either barren or had been rotated with dry grass that was brown and patchy. End-less stretches of brown or brown-yellow, an occasional wet ditch, and dipping telephone lines along the roadside. The sky was a sheet of gray, and it felt like it might snow.

I stopped the second night near dusk at a low, flat, pink motel made of cinder blocks where two roads intersected. Six rooms in a row with a white farmhouse at one end, some out-buildings next to it, a gravel parking lot, and an empty swimming pool with juniper bushes between the house and the rooms. There was a big tree on one side of the house whose barren branches hung over a corner of the pool.

The foyer of the farmhouse served as the motel office. I rang the bell on the little desk next to the staircase. A middle-aged man came out of the kitchen wiping his hands on a dish-towel. Through the doorway, I could see the back of a woman standing at the kitchen sink, water running. They both had short salt-and-pepper hair.

He didn't ask if I wanted a room, but took out a small card and a pen from the desk and set them down in front of me. I filled out the card and put the amount of money noted on top of it while he sorted through a cigar box of keys. He handed me one.

"I can't remember my license plate number. Want me to go and look?" I said.

"Nope," he said. "I gave you the end room, the one farthest away from the highway. Have you eaten?"

I shook my head.

"Well, if you're looking for something to do, you can go into Carson. There's a diner there might still be open and a pizza place. Else we can fix you up a sandwich or something."

"Sandwich suits me fine," I said.

"Won't be fancy." He looked out the window past me at the gray sky that had grown pink on the horizon. "I like to sit outside a while this time of night, watch the light change. If it's not too cold for you, go get settled and come out by the pool. I'll bring your food out there."

I said thanks and drove over to the room. It was clean and spare. I washed up, put on a coat, and went back outside. He was sitting in one of the two rusty tulip-backed chairs next to the pool holding a plate and a brown mug from which steam curled. He watched me come across the cinder parking lot and sit down next to him. Then he handed me the food and set the mug next to me on the concrete.

"My wife made that chicken salad and the pie," he said. "It's pretty good."

"Thanks," I said. I took a bite of the sandwich and looked at it. "That's great."

He nodded and looked out across the highway where the horizon had a purple line drawn between the gray and pink. A barn stood silhouetted in the front of the field across from us, and a flock of widely dispersed blackbirds flew through the hue over the stand of trees at the back of it.

"Is there a river back there?" I gestured with the sandwich where he was gazing.

"Creek," he said, pronouncing it "crick." "Brook. Stream. Whatever you want to call it. Isn't big enough to be called a river. Sometimes brings enough water to irrigate, that's about all."

I looked at the side of him and took a sip of tea. His face needed shaving. The outsides of his eyelids drooped, and his lips were pressed together in a short, thin mark. There were large calluses on both of his palms where they met his fingers. He held his hands in his lap, sat back and rubbed his thumbs together slowly. I thought he was perhaps ten years older than me, somewhere in his mid-fifties.

"You farm any of this?" I asked.

"Used to," he said. He swept his hand in an arc. "Just about all of it at one time. Sold it off little by little. We had no kids to help, to pass it on to. Built this fly-by operation a few years back and sold everything but a couple acres next to the house where we keep a garden and a horse. That's it."

"Place doing all right?"

"You're the only paying customer right now." He chuckled. "Summer, we get a little better business. It's at this crossroads, you see. Truth is, most folks use the interstate nowadays. Thought about putting in a filling pump, maybe a lunch counter–type deal to help drum up business, but I don't know. Truth is, it hasn't worked out to be quite as lucrative as we'd hoped. Time goes on, and it doesn't make as much sense as it used to." He shrugged. "We get by."

I nodded, but he wasn't looking at me. I stared out where he was: fencing and barren land in every direction. An eighteen-wheeler rumbled by from the north. It was the first vehicle that had passed since I'd sat down. Then a tiny, thin cloud of dust rose from the back of the field behind the barn, and in front of it an old truck snaked slowly toward us.

"Kate," he said quietly.

"That truck?"

We watched the ribbon of smoke drift after the truck for a moment. Then he pointed and said, "That barn burned down last spring. Struck by lightning. Course, we all got together, raised them a new one. Then worse yet, her husband dies at the equinox. Some kind of aneurysm." He shook his head.

"She's had an awful time of it. Trying to keep up the farm and the kids on her own."

The truck kept along. I ate the warm pie, and we watched. The sky was muted now, gray-purple toward the truck and the rest of it going dark. A few stars had crept out. The truck came up the last rise and alongside the barn. A woman with brown hair, jeans, and a jean jacket climbed out, followed by a tow-headed boy and girl in too big sweat shirts. She waved once to the man next to me, then dragged open the big barn doors, and the children followed her inside. A cream-colored light filled the barn's windows, as well as the patch of dirt in front of the open doors.

"Feeding time," the man said softly.

We watched the coal-like figures of cows lumbering slowly in from the field in the gathering darkness. Now our breath hung in short cloud blasts. I sipped tea and held the mug in both hands to warm them.

After a few moments, Kate came out of the barn and walked up to the fence across the shallow gully next to the roadside. She put her arms on top of one of the posts.

"Say, Rudy," she called. "I could use a hand with something, if you got a minute."

He stood up.

"Can I help?" I said.

"Come along, if you want. Maybe she needs something lifted."

We walked across the highway, between the barbed wire strands, and stood in front of her in the soft, crumbling earth. Kate's skin was either wind or sun darkened, but it didn't hurt the way she looked. She nodded to me, and I nodded back.

"Yearling's got her head stuck," she said.

"Let's go see," Rudy said.

The big clumps of dirt broke softly and easily under our feet. The collective low moans of the approaching cows mingled with the quiet voices inside the barn. When we stepped into the light, I could see her children up in the hayloft holding toy cars.

There were perhaps twenty open slats low on the far side of the barn. The trough on the inside of the slats was full of the new hay she'd spread. The muzzles of most of the cows chewed hay from outside, in the barnyard on the other side of the slats. But in the slat closest to the barn door, a yearling's small head had come all the way through the boards and was tossing awkwardly in the hay. The sound from it reminded me of a bleat from a sheep being shorn. We walked up to it.

"There she is," Kate said. "That gap's been fine for all the rest. No problems."

Rudy nodded and smiled. "Well, she isn't happy with things right now, is she? Let's get her out." He brushed a strand of hay from the yearling's eye, which looked up at him big and terrified. "Go out in the yard and hold her rear end. When I say so, sit her down."

Although he hadn't asked me specifically, I followed Kate through the gate and into the black mud of the barnyard. We stood behind the yearling. The cold night sky had filled with stars. Steam rose off the backs of the cows. Tails swished around us, and the smell of dung was sweet in the back of my nose. We glanced at each other.

"Ready?" Rudy asked.

"Yes," Kate answered and set her hands on the yearling's hind flank. I did the same on my side.

Through the slats, we watched Rudy slowly lower one hand under the yearling's muzzle and close the other over it. He held his hands firmly together and told her, "Shh." Then he gently turned the yearling's head so she looked straight ahead and lifted it. Her hooves pawed the muck. One of the other cows began to urinate, a steady, steam-filled, forceful stream.

"All right," Rudy said slowly. "Easy now. Stand away from her legs. Set her rump down toward the end of the yard. Easy."

We did, and he helped the yearling's head back through the slats. Her ears folded over on themselves, then she was out, running clumsily on her spindly legs to the end of the yard. Kate looked at me and smiled.

"Thanks," she said.

I nodded. She wiped her palms on the front of her jeans, and then I followed her around to the open doorway of the barn. Rudy was tossing new hay into the depression where the yearling's head had been. Kate walked up to him and patted his shoulder twice.

"Appreciate that," she told him.

"Gwen's made pie," he said. "You and the kids want some, come over."

"Wish we could," she said. "Getting late though. School night."

A toy car fell out of the loft into the sawdust near my feet. I handed it back up to the boy, who had his mother's big, gentle eyes. I looked at her, and those eyes smiled again.

"All right then," I heard Rudy say.

I held her gaze as long as I dared, then followed him back through the field, under the fencing, and across the highway to the motel.

He picked up the plate and mug, and we stood next to the tulip-backed chairs. It was quiet. The soft white light from the kitchen came across the lower part of the big tree and threw shadows on that corner of the empty pool. A broken branch sat among the wet leaves on the blue cement bottom. The light also crossed the side of Rudy's face, darkening it. He extended his hand, and I shook it. He went back inside, and I walked around the pool to my room, listening to their storm door swing slowly shut behind him.

Later in the night, I heard a train go by quite a ways off through the fields to the north. Perhaps, I remember thinking, I could get to know her, and maybe other things would develop from there. But I didn't see how. I'd been alone a long time.

Every now and then, a truck or a car went by in one of the four directions. Otherwise, it was still, except for a few birds that started tittering toward daybreak.

*

I stopped at the diner in Carson that next morning for breakfast. It was just a narrow place on a corner with a short counter and a couple of booths. Two men in work caps and plaid, long-sleeved shirts sat across from one another at the back booth, and a waitress was pouring coffee at the end of the counter for an old man with a toothpick between his lips. They all stopped and watched me as I settled onto a stool near the cash register.

The waitress came over, set a cup in front of me, and filled it with coffee. She was a solid woman with a friendly face and glasses. I ordered eggs and toast, and she called that through a little window behind her. It was warm. I unbuckled my coat.

The two men went back to talking quietly. The old man and I nodded at each other and then turned back to our coffee. Smells from the spitting grill came from the kitchen.

The waitress set a napkin and silverware in front of me. I asked her, "How many people live here?"

She paused and then said, "I don't rightly know. Frank, how many people live in Carson?"

The old man regarded her, chewing on his toothpick. "In the county or within the city limits?"

I shrugged. He switched the toothpick to the other side of his mouth and considered some more. Finally he said, "About fifteen hundred here in town…suppose about two thousand across the county. It's a big county, bigger than you realize."

"Seems like a nice place," I told them.

"Just right," she said.

The old man nodded and turned back to his coffee. I did the same. A few minutes later, the waitress put my breakfast in front of me. I ate slowly. I had no particular timetable to meet except to be at my cousin's house in Omaha before he went to bed that night. It was a long drive, most of it, I knew, mile after mile through empty fields.

After a while, the two men at the booth stood up, pulled coats on, and shuffled out the door. Bells on it tinkled when they opened and closed it. As I was pushing my empty plate away, the bells tinkled again, and Kate came in with her two kids. I swallowed.

"Hey," the waitress said to them and smiled.

"Morning, Mabel," Kate told her. She glanced at me and smiled. I did the same, then fiddled with the handle on my coffee cup. "Hey, Frank," she said.

The old man nodded. "Kate."

Mabel took the lid off a little pedestal on the back counter, put two sugar donuts in a small white bag, and brought it to them at the cash register. She gave the bag to the boy. He and his sister each hung to opposite corners of their mother's jean jacket.

"There you go, darlings," Mabel told them and grinned. Kate handed her some money.

"Fixing to snow?" Mabel asked.

"Feels like it," Kate said.

They nodded at each other slowly until Mabel asked, "Kids okay?"

"Oh, little one has the sniffles. They're fine."

Kate ruffled her daughter's hair. Mabel nodded some more. The radio came on low in the kitchen: a country-western song. Someone switched the stations before settling on a news program giving a report on grain prices.

"Well," Kate said. "School's going to start."

Mabel wiped her hands on her apron and said, "You all have a good day now." I watched her push through the swinging door into the kitchen.

When I turned, Kate was smiling quietly at me again. She stood for a moment like that. "Thanks again for your help last night," she said.

"Sure."

We looked at each other some more until she raised her eyebrows, sighed, and said, "Well."

Then she turned and went back out through the tinkling diner door. I watched her go down the sidewalk with a hand on the shoulder of each of her kids. The boy swung the donut bag as he went. I swallowed again, shook my head. I took another sip of coffee and felt my heart thudding away. I kicked the base of the counter, and Frank glanced over at me. I put some money on the counter and left quickly.

But the street was empty, no sign of their truck. I walked up to the corner, and the side street was vacant too, in both directions. A calico cat sauntered out from behind the gas station across the street, crossed the blacktop, and stopped in front of me, its tail standing straight up. The tail swayed back and forth. After a moment, it purred once, then went off up the sidewalk and into the alley behind the diner. I don't know if it had stopped to be petted or not. Either way, I'd chosen not to, and so off it had gone, on its way. Not much chance I'd ever see it again.

*

I worked for that cousin for about a year. Winter was pretty long and hard in Omaha, not much to do. I started collecting pennies, and that passed some of the hours outside of work. The library had a pretty good periodical section, so I spent time there. I took long walks along the river, had lots of opportunity to think about things.

After my cousin's business went under, I stayed a while longer and took a job sheetrocking for an outfit that was building a new strip mall. But that ended too, so I eventually decided to head back to Seattle to see if I could find a ship to put out on again. I was in no rush, so drove by way of Carson.

I stopped at the crossroads motel. It stood closed up, empty, patches of weeds littering the cinder lot, plywood up in some of the farmhouse windows. The tulip-backed chairs were gone, so I sat on the front step of the farmhouse. It was a warm late-spring afternoon, several hours before dusk. The wood on the barn across the road had weathered and darkened. The field behind it was planted in ankle-high new corn. I watched a tractor motor back and forth toward the road among the rows that were planted horizontal to it. From that distance, I couldn't tell who was driving. Its approach was gradual. In order to pass the time, I tossed gravel at the mailbox that stood on a crooked post where the parking lot met the road. I made myself breathe slowly.

Gradually I could make out the driver with his tangle of red hair: a gangly high school–aged boy. At one point, as he was working the nearest row of corn, he raised his hand in greeting from the cab of the tractor. I did the same. I waited until he'd pulled up in front of the barn before I walked across the road and through the barbed wire. He'd opened the barn doors. There were no cows in the yard, and the feed trough was empty of hay. I saw some thrashing blades and other equipment in the sawdust under the loft.

The tractor stood idling. The boy came back around the side of it and stopped in front of me. "Hi," he said. "Say, that motel is closed."

I nodded and asked, "Same lady own this place? Kate?"

He shook his head. "Nah, she sold to my uncle, moved away."

I didn't say anything, and neither did he. He squinted at me. I noticed that one of his two front teeth overlapped the other, but I wasn't thinking about that.

"Any idea where she went?" I asked.

"Nah. I don't think she said exactly. Somewhere with warmer winters, I know that."

I nodded some more. I looked out over the field where he'd been working, and he followed my gaze. There were several groups of blackbirds out over the low growth. He waved his hand passively toward them and said, "Shoo."

A dog barked somewhere. I could smell the diesel from the idling tractor. The boy put one foot up on the running board and said, "Well."

"Thanks, kindly," I said.

I turned and headed back toward the fence. I listened to the tractor chug into the barn, then the engine switch off as I crossed the road. I got back in my car, but didn't start it right away. I'd never been with anyone for more than a few weeks at a time, and that had only been on a couple of occasions years before. I'm not sure what I would have said if she'd still been there. I guess I would have thought of something. After that last time, I hoped so, anyway. I'd thought about it enough, I knew that.

Perhaps ten minutes passed before the boy came back out of the barn and closed its doors. He started walking up the long drive that Kate's truck had come down. I watched the back of him until he disappeared into the trees behind the field. Then I started the car and headed to wherever the next place was that I would hang my hat.

*

I spent the twenty-plus years that followed mostly shipping out here and there. Went to some interesting foreign ports, saw a good portion of the world, I guess you could say. I suppose I had my share of adventures. My back eventually got the best of me, and I settled in this town here in Minnesota where an old crewmate's family owned a hardware store. I went to work for them a decade or so ago and have been there since. It's not hard on my back, and it's work I like well enough. With only Social Security, I have to augment a bit, so that fills the bill. Truth is, I need to work just to pass the time. I still have my coins. Plenty of places to walk. Friendly enough folks around. There's a library; I've begun reading histories and biographies. Brought home a cookbook once and tried a few recipes, but it was hard to get excited much making meals for one.

Besides that crossroads, there are plenty of other places I could have called home. Usually, I realize now, something small just felt right about them. I remember a little town along the boundary waters where Canada meets the Great Lakes, south of Route 2, distinguished in my mind by still black ponds, red dirt roads, and people moving at a sensible pace. There was a small city in the mountains of Mexico; the buildings there were as white as those in Greek villages, but the night air retained a sweet fragrance from the surrounding pines, and people greeted you quietly when you passed by.

Another is a place I paused to get gas one summer afternoon somewhere in Oregon. Across the street was a park that had green grass and tall willow trees that threw long, liquid shadows. In the back of the park, I could see the shimmer of a municipal pool in the clean light and hear the splash of water and the shouts of children. A big woman sat in a folding chair at the front of the park near the entrance. She was crocheting and selling huckleberry jam. The jars sat on a card table that had an umbrella fixed on it against the sun.

There are lots of other places, too many to mention. I could have called any of them: home. Yet, I never did. Those prior opportunities are gone. This will be my final resting place; circumstances pretty much dictate it, and that's all right. It's as good as any other. Nothing makes it stand apart, no clutch of the heart, but it's fine. It's home. Home, sweet home.

I don't know. You settle places, you fill your life with events and memories and things. Sometimes, though, I think it's those you omit that mean the most. At least in certain instances. At least in those that may always remain irretrievable. I'm not sure about much, but about that, I'm fairly certain.

Previously published in Ruminate *(2010)*

FAMILY RITES

A dozen Larsons gathered in the viewing room at Svensen's Funeral Home on State Street. Aunt Hazel, laid out in a
plain Protestant coffin, appeared predictably diminished and
waxen, but something was not right. She had been cosmetically
transformed into a composite image of her two sisters: part
schoolmarm, part church lady. Gone were the false eyelashes
and ruby red lipstick, the expertly tweezed eyebrows replaced
by dark patches that resembled mustaches. Her face was gaunt,
and the faint dusting of pink powder on her once full cheeks
did nothing to disguise her long battle with death. Aunt Louise
had insisted on a drab gray dress for her burial, a string of fake
plastic pearls around her neck. Sensible shoes, the kind Hazel
would never be caught dead in when she was alive, covered
her feet.

"Hazel—we all miss her so," crooned Louise, who had re-
fashioned herself into a grotesque parody of her dead sister.
She wore enough makeup for a dozen chorus girls, and the
contours of her thin lips were clownishly distorted with garish

red lipstick. The fur stole clutching her shoulders was seriously molting and smelled of mothballs, the beady glass eyes of two dead foxes sustaining a steady glare.

I seemed to be the only one who noticed her demented appearance. Blowing away bits of fur, I restrained myself from shouting: "This funeral is total bullshit. You were Hazel's goddamned sister, and you never once visited her when she was suffering. None of you did!"

But since I hadn't gone to see Hazel myself, I remained silent. I was in my twenties, and dying didn't interest me much. I was too busy starting my life to care about its conclusion. Truthfully, I had come back to St. Paul because I hoped to wheedle some cash from my folks, who from time to time had floated me a loan. I don't think they actually believed I would ever pay them back. We were all practiced at maintaining fictions.

After I left home for San Francisco, I worked at the Emporium department store near Union Square to support myself through art school. I made friends with several co-workers who reminded me of Aunt Hazel—fabulous, fun-loving single women who had struck out on their own and enjoyed their share of gentlemen admirers. They introduced me to the bars in the Tenderloin, drag bars mostly, where they seemed to fit right in.

This was in the 1970s, not exactly an innocent time, but less complicated, less infused with consequences than now. You could go missing then, leave home and just disappear. I was a good son though, or at least that was the myth the family perpetuated. I called home whenever I thought of it and even returned for Christmas. It was my mother who told me that Hazel had cancer. She had died alone in a Chicago hospital, her body shipped to St. Paul for a service and burial.

My father picked me up at the airport. I'd gotten my hair cut short to curtail criticism and increase my chances of receiving a loan.

"Did you bring anything to wear for tomorrow's funeral?" Dad asked.

"Not really." I'd packed my suitcase with a jumble of clothes that needed washing: a couple pairs of torn jeans, a few rock band T-shirts, and two ratty wool sweaters picked up from the Mission Goodwill for the Minnesota winter weather. "Maybe I shouldn't go."

"Don't turn your nose up at funerals. Everyone dies eventually." I couldn't tell if Dad was being philosophical or making a joke.

Dad took me upstairs after the usual fusillade of hugs, kisses, and tears from my mother. "Here, try these on." He pulled a dark suit from his closet, a size too large for me, and handed me a white shirt with ring around the collar, along with a striped tie. I stared at it as if it were flattened roadkill. The last time I'd worn a tie was at my high school graduation. Peering in the mirror as I attempted to comb my hair into a part, I was shocked to see how straight and corporate I appeared, the very image of the person I had left home to escape.

*

Aunt Hazel escaped the family farm at seventeen and made a living performing acrobatics on the wings of biplanes at county fairs. Later, in the 1950s, she appeared in a photograph on the front page of the *Miami Herald,* surrounded by certain underworld figures. County fair aerialist, a favorite of gangsters and mayors, she was ostracized by the family for good after they learned that a prominent Chicago businessman had installed her in a Michigan Avenue hotel. The family grapevine hissed with the word "mistress."

The first time I saw my aunt was at a family reunion, a potluck picnic in a rustic state park outside of St. Paul. I was ten; I remember because that was the summer of my first sexual experience—with my classmate Larry Sorensen, who became Svensen's funeral director.

Hazel arrived, uninvited, in yellow taxi on a hot, humid, and very tedious afternoon. She emerged from the back seat regally wrapped in a leopard-skin jacket and wearing enough jewelry to slow down a gazelle.

"They're not real gems," snapped Aunt Louise, as if that explained everything.

Hazel stepped along the dirt path a bit wobbly in her heels, the scent of her perfume preceding her. Her coppery hair shone from underneath a white feather hat, her emerald green silk dress shimmering in the sunlight. She was the epitome of elegance and sophistication among habitués of JC Penney and Sears Roebuck.

A bolt of excitement suddenly took hold of the bucolic scene. Uncle Harry, rapt and feral, bolted up from the picnic table and rushed over to assist her procession. My father, humming faintly, popped open another can of Hamm's and took several deep gulps. Even my little brother Jamie and our pack of noisy cousins stopped playing on the slide and swing set to stare.

Hazel greeted each of her startled relatives, holding out her hand as if it were meant to be kissed, her grand manner a reminder that she hadn't forgotten their roles in her expulsion.

I was still a child, but felt an affinity with her brilliant stage-craft and rejoiced that she was banishing my boredom. Mother, an English teacher who possessed a romantic streak, gave me a conspiratorial glance. She had always reserved a muted admiration for her sister despite her flamboyance and waywardness, or maybe because of it. Harry offered Hazel a paper cup of table wine. It spilled down the back of my shirt when she hugged me. It was like a baptism. I made everyone scoot down so she could sit next to me on the picnic bench. Dad grabbed a paper plate and loaded it up with fried chicken, baked beans, and potato salad, avoiding the pickled herring.

Aunt Louise, mortally affronted, tried to put up a good front. Smiling tightly, she asked Hazel a few neutral questions. "How are you? Was your trip taxing? How did you find out where we were?" Hazel answered amiably, embellishing her replies. She explained that she was in town only for the day, scandalously adding that she had accompanied her "friend," the one who was rumored to pay for her suite at the Palmer House, for an important business conference. Just before they left Chicago, he had surprised her with the gift of the leopard jacket.

The men licked their lips as they drank in every word. Uncle Harry blurted out something suggestive: "Does your boyfriend order up room service when he visits?" Louise cut him with a withering look.

The taxi reappeared barely half an hour after her entrance. Hazel announced that she was expected back in town for cocktails. I fantasized what it would be like to be her and have cocktails with a boyfriend. I jumped at the chance to accompany her to the cab, an imperial consort in thrall with the lush scent of her perfume, which she told me was called Eternity.

Hazel bent down and kissed me on the cheek. "You're a clever boy. Don't let them wear you down." With those enigmatic words, she disappeared inside. I watched as the taxi crunched down the gravel road and vanished behind a stand of elm trees.

I returned to the table, downcast. Louise was whispering in my mother's ear. My father and Uncle Harry looked stricken, glancing at one another covertly.

"Well. Thank God that's over with," declared Louise. "Anyone for rice pudding?"

*

Sacred Muzak burbled from speakers in the viewing room at Svensen's Funeral Home. A vanload of lilies and orchids filled the room, sent by an old admirer of Hazel, a scion from a Milwaukee brewing family. A jungle of exotic blooms surrounded the mourners shrouded in black, releasing a heavenly scent that reminded me of Eternity.

"Hazel would have to show off like this, wouldn't she!" complained Aunt Louise, her makeup cracking and lipstick smeared into a horizontal slash.

I picked a delicate white blossom from an orchid plant and pushed it into the buttonhole of my borrowed suit coat.

There was no church funeral, only a short service with no eulogies, as if the family scandal should always remain a secret. Afterward, the bereaved congregated in the lobby over weak coffee and day-old pastries. Larry Sorensen, the funeral director who was all grown up now, studiously avoided talking to me.

Aunt Louise's voice resonated like static above the murmuring of the others. "Hazel may have once lived on the top floor of a fine hotel, but then her businessman died and his family contested the will. She had to work as a waitress and take a studio apartment in a seedy part of town. She died all alone, poor soul. Well, I suppose we all reap what we sow."

Stealing back into the viewing room, I took the bloom from my buttonhole and placed it on Hazel's waist. I stared at the mole above her mouth and felt her breath, like butterfly wings brushing against my face. I leaned in closer and heard her whisper: "We're alike, you and I, birds of a feather. You did the right thing leaving the nest. Don't ever doubt it, honey."

My parents appeared, letting me know they were leaving. There was talk of a blizzard. I passed by Larry at the door and gave him an exaggerated wink.

We rode in silence all the way home, watching the first snow flurries of the season hit the windshield, each of us buried in our own thoughts, our own fictions.

Poetry
by Mbeke

WE WOMEN WHO TRAVEL FAR

We women who travel far
Not needing man, woman or car
We women who go away
Feel the fear and still go and slay
We take our lives and we leave
The adventure keeps us going
We walk where lions tread
Hiking, singing and skateboarding
We wear the traditional dress
Loving creativity and expression
We eat foods from far-off lands
And learn the meaning of their religion
Many of us are spiritual
Our travels have broken down barriers
We are not afraid of new places

Embracing the challenge like warriors
We know they don't know us
Asking always, "Where are you from?"
Making crazy and wild assumptions
That continue to make us strong.
Personal relationships are challenged
It's the price that the distance brings
Finding love along the journey?
Is not a straightforward thing!!!
Most of us still continue
For this is the life we have chosen
It brings quality in abundance
As things can always smell of roses
It's a life that's not for all
Some need the space in which they were born
Others have planted seeds
Moving and sprouting like grains of corn.
My Ode to my sisters
Who take their lives and start anew
May your journeys be love filled
As you grow your world mind view.

AMERICA

Only home I've ever known.
Where I learned to walk, and speak, and dream, and smile

and see ma momma cry.
It is the where to my confusions,

cutting beneath my skin,

hating the brown Nahuatl I have within.
America.

The dream to my people that see heaven when they hear that
7-letter word.
The hope that we feel when we think of it,
And the illusion that we carry when we see those 50 stars,

hoping we can earn just 1.
Yet we didn't know that as we step in those 13 lines,
We suddenly are mojados.
We are the bad hombres roaming the streets

and the beaners cleaning your yards,
And eventually spics and illegals,

raping and dealing and doing the inhumane.
When in reality, the inhumane is done to the human.
Our people get taken away because we are lazy and because
we are "extraterrestrials"
We are the walking proof of criminal and dangerous,

because the color of our skin is darker than your white,

and the dark brown I hold is a threat to your Manifest Des-
tiny.

Great excuse by the way.

America.
The journey that kills us and breaks us, and devours our humanity,

stepping into our dignity, chaining us to ILLEGAL.

Yet it is where our tacos are celebrated,
And the white man carries a big sombrero with "*Viva Mex-
ico.*"
It is where white is okay, but brown, black or tan is not.
It is where rich is gifted and poor is failure.
It is where privilege is power and people is weakness.

It is The Who, crushing my dream and shouting at me:

"Give up Jose. Give up Maria.

Give up you orange picker, beaner, wetback.

Give up mamacita, curvy one.

Give up ILLEGAL and go back to your damn country."
Country.

America.
The dream that nourished my hopes,
But killed the beauty of my culture,
Planting anxiety on my shoulder, waiting to penetrate a tattoo
name that will be "deported."

Ohhhh, but don't worry, I'll be greater than El Chapo,
Ballin' w the cash chopping heads like a macho
Laced up in my couch eating some burritos and some tacos
Plotting the next cartel with ma fucking vatos… right?

See,

Reason I came here was because
This country was my dream. This country was my mom's
dream.
This country is our people's dream.
Where liberty and freedom is welcome and exploitation is
caged away.
But continues to be a location, where my Latinx history is
forgotten.
Where the bodies of my people shed blood to the American
Flag
Assimilating our Fortaleza to their benefit.
Criminalizing the beautiful brown melanin that I hold so
dear.

White boy. White girl.
America es mi pinche sueño.
Es mi hogar y es mi identidad.

It is where my Spanish and Aztec is welcome and my raza
will luchar
It is where I am native and not the immigrant, because USA
is my homeland too.
Unlike you, white boy, I welcome the hungry and the poor.
WE, NATIVE.
welcome the immigrant and the ones in need.
Because we built America.
Nosotros somos America.
*Somos cabrones y orgullosos. Y esta tierra Mijos, nos pertenece a no-
sotros.*

So let me tell you something, privilege,
America is the dream that will not die and the reality that will
occur.
It will be where our shoulders are clean,

not worrying about who in your family could be taken away.
Not your mother. Not your sister. Not your brother. Not
your cousin.

Not one more.

No more worries, my child, you no longer will live in the
shadows.

You no longer will hide and pretend you are white.

You no longer will have to worry in the back of your mind

about your future being taken away while sitting in your math
class.

No.

You no longer will have to worry about your people screaming "*La Migra*"

Don't worry, child, because America is YOUR home.
America, *estoy en casa.*

WHERE ARE YOU REALLY FROM?

"Where are you really from?"

I am the youngest of six and the only one in my family not born in China. Instead, I was conceived and oriented in Duluth, Minnesota. As a Chinese-American it took me quite a while to realize just how much weight that little hyphen carried. My father owned Joe Huie's Café, a typical chop suey joint, but it was images of pop culture that fed, formed, and confused me. The everyday realities of my family and myself were seldom reflected in that visual landscape, to the point that my own parents seemed foreign and exotic, while I became a stranger and a riddle to myself.

This is my first-grade class picture. Do you see me? Do I stick out? Throughout much of my public education, I was the only Asian student, not just in my class, but in the entire school. It wasn't until high school that another Asian kid showed up, and when I saw him, I avoided him. I don't think I realized at the time I was avoiding someone just because he kind of looked like me. I didn't want to think about it. It wasn't until twenty years later, well into adulthood and my photography career, that I started to confront my "ethnocentric" filter.

What am I? I was confronted with this question early on when my fellow Duluthians asked, "Where are you from?" To which I replied, with as little annoyance as possible, "Duluth." Then the inevitable follow-up question: "No, where are you really from?" Some folks are just trying to be friendly, but this is what that question usually implied: "Because of what you look like, you are not one of us. So what are you?"

I have come to realize that for most of my adolescence, I thought I was like everyone else. I read the same books, watched the same TV shows and Hollywood movies. But you don't grow up with a mirror in front of you. The people around you are your mirror. You are what you see. I had forgotten what I looked like, so when I saw this other Asian in high school, I was really seeing myself for the first time.

When I was twenty, I bought my first camera, a Minolta SLR. A couple of years later, I earned my BA in journalism, intending to become a reporter. But after taking a one-week workshop from the iconic street photographer Garry Winogrand, I decided to become a street photographer. Since then I have photographed thousands of people throughout my career, most of them strangers, and the underlying questions in all of my projects are, "Who are we?" and "Who gets to define who we are?"

Excerpted and condensed from Chinese-ness: The Meanings of Identity and the Nature of Belonging, *published by the Minnesota Historical Society Press*

Memoir
by Grace T. Andreoff Smith and Alicia Smith

I AM FROM PITKAS POINT, ALASKA

I told Alicia, she started it, she is involved, and she has to be my right hand.

I am Grace T. Andreoff Smith. I am Yupik. I am from Pitkas Point, Alaska. I have seven kids and eleven grandchildren. Alicia is number three.

Alicia came home one day and said, "Mom, we are starting a fundraiser for you to go back home." I haven't been home for over fifty years. Nobody there knew where I went. Alicia and her co-workers started fundraising for me to go back to Alaska. Truthfully, I became very angry and scared, and I didn't know what to say. I did not expect to ever go back to my hometown.

"Lishi, you started it, and you are coming with me," I said. "I am not going up there by myself." I asked my kids, who wanted to come with? Two of my other daughters, Elizabeth and Sarah, and a friend of Alicia's came with. I said I need strength. I was so mad, I would start praying. In praying, I said, "God, ancestors, and grandfather, mom, dad, and big brother, I don't know if I can handle that. I don't know if I want to go back to everything that I ran away from." And I kept praying, offered tobacco, and asked for strength.

Before the trip, I had a whole year of going through a lot of healing. A lot of anger. A lot of the time I couldn't cry. I didn't cry. I just yelled. But I knew I finally had to face the truth.

I have not been in my hometown since my parents died. My mom and dad died of TB. I'm the only survivor of TB. The only family I have is my seven kids and my eleven grandchildren. I said, what am I going to do? But I kept hearing from Alicia that I was going to go through a lot of healing. Together we are going to see where my mom and dad were buried.

We made the reservations to go. I called Pitkas Point. The person I talked to was one of my cousins. He had a lodge where my girls and I could stay. I asked if they had cars to rent, and they did. When we got on the plane and landed in Seattle, we ended up sleeping on the floor of the airport because we had eight hours of waiting there. Finally, we got on the plane to go to my hometown.

We got to Saint Mary's, which is right by Pitkas Point. This woman came up to me and said, "Are you Grace Andreoff?" Nobody has said my maiden name for years.

"I used to be Andreoff, I am Smith now," I said.

And she said to me, "You are tall."

"Yes."

"You have gained weight."

"Yes, I did." And I said, "What is your name?" I didn't recognize her because we have aged. She told me her name was Esther. She was one of my best friends. I thought, Wow!

It started raining. It was a gentle rain. And it rained the whole seven days we were there. And somebody said, "It's your ancestors crying; they are happy that you came back home."

*

We asked Billy, the relative who we rented the cabin and car from, how we could get to Pitkas Point. He told us how. I was scared. I told one of my daughters that she had to drive.

When we got there, we went to the Russian Orthodox Church. To be in the Russian Orthodox Church after more than fifty years gave me the same feeling I had when I was small. The memory of my dad holding me and carrying me to the altar for me to have the chalice and little bread—that memory came back.

That is what my family was. The graveyards had flooded so bad that a lot of the graves were floating down the river. I was looking, and I thought: I wonder if my mom and dad's grave went down the river?

We talked to the pastor. I wanted to see two people, Natalia and Willie, because I used to watch them and babysit them. One of the pastor's kids took us to Willie's house. We met him, and I said, "Wow, I am taller than you." I put my arms around him and him on me. I said, "I don't think you remember me. You were about three or four years old when I left."

I asked him to take us to his sister Natalia's house. We walked in, and I said, "I don't think you remember me."

"I do remember you," she said.

And that just hit me: Even though she was so young when I left, she still remembered me.

"Hold on," she said. Her sister Thelma went to the organizer on the wall, took out an envelope, and handed it to me.

You could tell it was a very old envelope. I opened it, and there it was my and my brother's birth certificates.

"How in the world did you guys save this?" I said.

My cousin Virginia—Thelma and Willie's as well as Natalia's mom, who has since passed away—was like a big sister to me. They had saved it all these years. And I thought, oh my gosh.

I thought about my brother. I wished he could have been there with me to visit Mom and Dad in our hometown, but he died. He had TB.

*

After my mom and dad died, my cousin sent my brother and me and one other cousin to boarding school, Holy Cross. I have not been able to say that name for years. Holy Cross.

It took a long time to go from Pitkas Point to Holy Cross; I don't know how many days. I don't know how old we were. I don't remember eating anything, but I do remember being scared.

When we got to Holy Cross, the guy said to go up there to the big white building. I can still picture the building. When we got into the building, I had never seen so many white people. I had only seen my people before. I was trying to figure out how come they were dressed so weird and in black and white. That always puzzled me.

The nuns took me and my brother and washed us in kerosene. I screamed and I yelled, saying, "It hurts!"

"Stop crying," she said. "We are killing all of the bugs out of you."

I didn't quite understand because I knew I had no bugs on me.

Our bed was downstairs in the engine room. No blankets, we just slept on the floor. I didn't quite understand what was going on. But at the same time, I was happy my brother was with me. He was my protection. He was my guide and my strength.

Like in the pictures you see, they cut my hair like that. And that was the style of the boarding school. And when I would talk, the nun would say, "Speak English." But they never taught me how to speak English. How I learned, I don't know. It is mainly a blur.

That is how my whole childhood was: a blur. Not being able to remember. But I do remember them hitting me on the hand with a ruler. And if I was speaking my language, I would have my hair pulled. The sister would say, "Quit speaking that barbarian language." I would have my ear pulled, and a big bar of soap would be rubbed in my mouth. I just couldn't understand why they couldn't hear what I was saying. I just was trying to figure out, where are we? Who are these people? Why are they getting mad at me? Why do they always hit me? Why are they always so mean to me? Why aren't they teaching me English?

Going to school was hard because I couldn't read. And when you couldn't, that was when you got beat. They beat you up, and you started crying and screaming. And they would say, "I will give you something to cry about!" They would hit me harder and harder, and I would cry and scream. The more you cry, the harder they hit you. I finally was able to hold back tears and not scream and cry. So I held back, not crying. Even to this day, I can't cry; it's too hard. Every time I am going to cry, I hear those nuns saying, "You are nothing but a barbarian savage."

Truthfully, I am surprised I am still alive after all the hitting, slapping, hair pulling, and getting beat up so bad my nose bled. I would say, "My nose is bleeding, my nose is bleeding!" and they would continue. They had those long sleeves, and they would roll them up. The more I yelled, "My nose is bleeding! My head hurts!" the harder they would hit. I had to force myself to stop crying. I was thinking, what did I do wrong?

They would talk about God. And I was thinking, they say how God loves you—I don't understand that. If God loves me, why am I being treated like this? I thought, their God must be different because you don't go around saying God loves you and give beatings.

The one soup that I cannot eat is broccoli soup. When they made it, they made me sit there until I finished the whole bowl of soup. I would be throwing up, and they would have me eat the soup. I couldn't understand. Now I know I was allergic to it.

And the stuff we had to do so they could take pictures of how happy we were. We had to run to Mother Superior, and those who didn't do it the right way were pulled off. I was one of them. I thought, I don't want to run to her; she is not nice to me. So I got pulled out by the hair.

I remember one time when we were out walking in the woods, I had to go to the bathroom because I had the runs. And I told the nun, "I have to go to the bathroom, I am going to have the runs, I have to go."

She just looked at me and said, "Get in the line."

"I have to go," I said. And all of the sudden, all down my clothes and legs, I had the runs.

She just looked at me and said, "You are staying in those clothes."

And those were the memories, a lot of memories, I did not want to remember.

That's how we lived in the boarding school. There are a lot of other memories. I am scared, it hurts, and people wonder why we cannot talk about boarding schools. They took away my personality, my culture, my language, but they did not break my spirit. Because I would fight inside. I said, I will be better; I will be better than what they are. I will love my children, I will listen to them. They would say, "Your people do not know how to raise kids and take care of kids. You don't know how to live like we do." I didn't quite understand that.

To be removed from your family and sent to a strange place. Not knowing the culture or what is going on. Forgetting about ancestors and relatives: It was really hard. How did I make it through? We weren't treated as people or as a person or as a little kid. I felt like I was treated like cattle: move here, move there. To this day if I see a nun, I go nuts. I feel like I am an animal caged, trying to figure out what is going on, what is going on.

I did a lot of praying to survive what I went through. One day I went outside, and I said, "God, you said you made me. All you did was take me to this place and say, this is where you are going to stay. Why do you have to do that to me?"

*

The school separated girls from boys, which meant that Matthew and I lived, ate, slept, learned, and were disciplined and traumatized in separate wings of the building. Late one night I could hear my brother crying out for help; locked doors and pitiless staff kept me away from comforting him. Matthew was eventually placed in isolation at a hospital.

A few days later a nun appeared in my room. She thrust a small cardboard box at me, saying, "Here are your brother's things."

"Did Matt send them to me?" I asked.

She just looked at me and said, "He died." She walked away.

Everything went blank. I don't know how long I was blank. That is how we lived: blank. Matthew died one day before his fifteenth birthday.

*

A lot of blanks happened in my life. Some of the stuff came back when I visited my hometown.

Every day we were taken to places. We went down to Mountain Village, and I happened to come across a woman who I went to boarding school with at Holy Cross. She started telling my girls how I got treated at the boarding school, and I didn't want my girls to hear it. I didn't want them to be ashamed of the way I got brought up at the boarding school. I went outside for "fresh air"—a cigarette, that's what I had.

She came out with me, and I said, "My kids didn't know I was in a boarding school."

"They have got to know," she said.

"It is really hard to talk about the boarding schools."

"You got the worst beating from the nuns. You were so small."

I didn't want to hear it anymore, and I said, "Please don't." The memories of what happened to me and other girls. Then to find out I got treated worse because I was so small.

"We would come up and say how are you doing?" she said. "Then you would smile and start laughing, and say I'm doing all right, and you would walk away. And that is when things got worse."

To share with my girls something I didn't want to remember, I felt so embarrassed. I thought my kids would be embarrassed about my family and my people because I kept hearing the nuns say that I am a barbarian and savage and I am no good. I didn't want my girls to be ashamed of me.

The girls said, "Mom, you have to go through the healing."

"It hurts, it hurts real bad," I said. "I don't want to remember. I did not want to go through that pain. I don't want to hear those nuns; I just don't want to hear that."

I told the girls and I told Kate, my cousin I lived with when I was younger at Mountain Village, that I got molested by the priest.

"Was that when we were living with Winifred?" Kate asked.

I said yes. Kate responded "Damn Winifred." That was a lot more healing. I couldn't understand: Why did he have to do that? All of us really trusted him and felt safe. All I could remember is a bed this high. He would put his knee on my back and say, "Stand up straight." I was trying to figure out why he was saying that. He'd start smiling. My mind went blank again.

I looked at Kate, and I said, "You know, I wish I had a wonderful childhood like you."

Maybe that is why I act like a kid all the time. Have fun, be crazy, and be joyful. And that is what we have to do—enjoy life. You may have a hard time, but life is precious. Our kids and our grandchildren are the best gifts that God has given me. I am so blessed.

I remember going to my cousin Art; they invited us to see his son and children. They showed us a picture on the refrigerator, a family picture. I looked at it and said, "I am angry. I am very angry."

I started yelling at my mom and dad and brother. "Why did you have to die? Why did you have to leave me? I've got no family picture of all of us! You had to leave me alone by myself!" I said I hate this. I said I am mad, and I am angry, and I am not going to apologize. And I just yelled at them for dying on me. Finally I said, "I know it wasn't your choice to die, but I missed out on my mother putting her arms around me and talking to me. I miss you because you weren't at my wedding. I miss you because you didn't see my firstborn and my grandchildren." I said, "I have nothing."

My kids said, "Mom, you've got us and the grandchildren." And those are my only family, my kids and my grandchildren.

That is why I didn't want to go back home. I didn't want those memories to come back.

But it was worthwhile. Something I had dreamt about for years, but it was so impossible. I was very thankful my girls were with me. The best part was to see my girls, how proud they were in my hometown. I showed them where my house used to be. I showed them the beach my brother and I used to run on and throw rocks. I said the only thing that is missing is all these dogs, the sled dogs. There were none.

The girls enjoyed it. Like Alicia said, we were city people. And I didn't realize how much of a city person I was until the girls and I were coming home from Pitkas Point, and we decided to get out of the car and start walking. All of a sudden I said we should go back. So we walked back to the car, and we told Art and Ruth where we were walking. "You were walking right toward a bear's den," Ruth said. I said, "Oh, my gosh!"

*

My kids asked me, "Where was your brother buried? Where did he die?"

"I don't know," I said. "I have no idea. I never knew where he was buried and what year he died."

One of my sons asked, "What hospital was he at?"

"Seward," I said. Matt died in Seward, Alaska. I think it was 1955, before he was fifteen.

My son checked it out. He found the cemetery and told me my brother was in lot A-15. He didn't have a gravestone to show who he was or how old he was, when his birthday was, when he died.

I got mad and said, "That is not right! That is not right! My brother was a human being. My brother has a name. He has a name!" I was so mad and upset because Matt was not remembered as a person or as a kid. He was just an alphabet and a number. You see, that is how we grew up in the boarding school: We had numbers that we had to write on our clothes.

About seven months ago, my son checked it out again, my brother's grave. Somebody had placed a gravestone for my brother, and whoever did that, I want to thank them. Now my brother has a gravestone.

The only thing I do know is when I go see my brother's grave, that is when I am going to break down and know how it is to cry.

*

A few years after my brother died, I met a family from Minnesota who was in search of live-in help. In 1959, I packed what few belongings I had, said goodbye to the Alaskan life I'd known, and moved to the Midwest. When I left Alaska, I was only a teenager, but I had already lived more and lost more than most people do in half a century.

Eventually I married and had a family. My children are my everything. With kids comes curiosity and the need for family history and identity. I wanted to go home for my children and my grandchildren. I want them to know where they're from. But I also wanted to do this for myself. I wanted to see where my parents are buried; I wanted to find my old home; I wanted to walk on the beach where the water comes up and where Matthew and I would play and fish and be together.

As the years went by, I realized I hadn't just left my home. I had left behind a sense of self: I was nothing; I had no place to belong.

This is what happened to us in boarding school. Our memories are gone. We have become what they wanted us to be.

That is how I felt until one day Alicia came home and said, "Mom, I found out that we've got a tribal name."

"We do?" I said.

"Yeah."

"What is it?"

"Yupik."

"We have to pick out our own tribal name?" I said.

"No, that is our tribal name."

All of a sudden the old shame came up again and all the time I wanted to be a person. I wanted to be somebody. It took me months to really accept it: I have a tribal name.

As we were leaving Pitkas Point to return to Minnesota, Father Isaacs said, "Have a safe trip home." Then he said, "Wait, have a safe trip back. Pitkas Point is your home."

I am very proud. I am Yupik. I am Pitkas Point, Alaska. That is where I became the person they took away from me. And I am a person. I am very proud to say I am Grace T. Andreoff Smith. I am Yupik, and I am from Pitkas Point, Alaska.

Photos by Emily Baxter. She is the founder/director of We Are All Criminals *(telling stories through photos)*
www.weareallcriminals.org

THRESHING

American Heritage Dictionary
thresh: verb. 1) to separate seed from a harvested plant mechanically; 2)
to strike repeatedly.

In these parts, most people get their news by word of mouth. Newspapers are consulted mainly for essential calendaring details and sports scores. For instance, today the front page of the *Union-Leader* lists Holy Week services for the Catholic and Lutheran churches. There's also a nice piece about Chief Gunderson's retirement party. But the big story is on how the Kenora Thistles claimed the Stanley Cup in a two-day rout over the Montreal Wanderers, thus striking a blow for small towns everywhere and fanning the dreams of the local schoolboys who are now sorry as heck to see winter recede.

But anybody with a little extra time on their hands this week might catch a short piece on the back page of the paper about the state mental hospital's two newest residents, Joe and Josephine Glodny. Wheat farmers with just a couple hundred acres, the Glodnys have generally kept to and relied on themselves, having no truck for busybodies, be they neighbors or government authorities. Instead, they've survived through hard work and harder prayer, a lot like the rest of the population in these parts. How they stood out, enough to bring forth the white coats and blue uniforms to apprehend them, was by being Polish and allowing the farm to fail. Naturally, suspicions were aroused that those two things were related.

It was maybe seven or eight years ago the family arrived in west-central Minnesota and set to farming. Their arrival was noted, but certainly not remarked upon beyond the usual:

"Seen there's a young couple making a go of it out by the Freiberg place."

"Yep." Pause.

"Pollacks."

"Yep." Pause.

"Not many Polanders around here."

"Nope." Big pause.

"Muriel says they speak English."

"That so?"

"Catholics, I suppose."

"You betcha."

March in Fergus Falls sometimes has the feel of a pause in the calendar. The first inklings of spring unsettle a collective winter catalepsy. As the geese return from their southern havens, the sound of small ice floes clattering from roofs is gradually replaced by the clomps of extra-large webbed feet on the shingles above. Bright-colored Christmas ornaments that dangled from trees on the German side of town get put away, and in their place painted Easter eggs are hung to drip. Out past the ball field and the hospitals, farmers prepare to plant a little corn, a little wheat, maybe a few sugar beets between the well-tended dairy pastures and hog stalls. The hogs are more agile this time of year, grunting as they plow their snouts into everybody's mud. Curious creatures, always hoping for something more to satisfy their appetites. The cows, in contrast, just stand and stare at folks, as if this year there might be something worth studying, but not really expecting it. The nearby Sauk River is ice free, about ready for canoes, and Watab Lake looks almost inviting enough to swim in. But there's mostly waiting and not a whole lot of action.

Fact is, this year it's been pretty quiet throughout the country and even most of the world. According to the local paper, the Ziegfield Follies are soon to open at the Jardin de Paris Theater in New York, not that any self-respecting Minnesotan would care to know. More pertinently, Henry Ford predicts that within a year, affordable automobiles will be available for purchase by every hardworking laborer in America. "Seeing is believing" is one common observation made in response around Fergus Falls supper tables. "Never take the place of a good team of horses" is another.

Maybe the lull in momentous events and newsworthy scandals explains the interest in the goings-on at the Glodny farm. Because until now, the Pollack farmers have not aroused much curiosity. In the eight years that the Glodnys have lived here, no priest or minister has ever visited their place, even to encourage worship on Sunday, and no neighbor ever happened to wander over with a welcoming casserole. The few times Joe stopped at a nearby farm in the early years to say *hey* and *like to make your acquaintance*, he spent an uncomfortable few minutes trying to engage in small talk with the resident landowner, whose sullen face stayed focused on the country ground, and who might've commented on the weather or feed prices, but not much else. Meanwhile, Josephine waited in vain to be invited into a front parlor, to be asked for news of the children, or to exchange pie recipes.

It's nothing personal. The Germans and Norwegians around here live by the gospel and tradition, and have a hard time imagining what outsiders have to offer. In fact, they have a hard time imagining anything at all. They see no point in chit-chat, far preferring familiar, silent company to stimulating conversation or novel ideas that go nowhere in particular.

Not that Germans and Norwegians, who settled here long ago, are *rude* or inhospitable. The Polish-Catholic Glodny kids go to school with the other children, and one of them has been seen playing baseball with the other boys. Merchants have always been cordial to the parents and perfectly willing to do business. Although never invited to join a church committee, Josephine was never actually turned away by one either, and not once was Joe refused service at a bar. It's just, on the street or at a social event—if the Glodnys were ever to be invited to one—it isn't likely that anyone would make eye contact or that a real conversation would get underway.

So the Glodnys kept to themselves on their small wheat farm. Maybe two years ago or so, the rumors got started, not blatant, of course, but sort of implied, that they'd come on hard times. It was after the family appeared at Roman services on Ash Wednesday to receive the cross of dust-to-dust on their foreheads. Outside the church Chip Obermann tried to make conversation with Joe. The Obermanns are Catholic only because Mrs. Obermann's Irish parents hold the deed to the family farm, an undeniably prosperous operation. Chip helps run his father's threshing ring. Being of the new generation, Chip can be a little brash, and maybe it appeared that way when, upon meeting Mr. Glodny on the church steps, he tipped his hat in a hello.

"Understand you're a wheat farmer, Mr. Glodny," Chip said.

"That's so," said Joe.

"Maybe we can talk business in the fall."

"Not likely."

"You work with the Larsson crew?" Chip asked.

"No."

"No? How do you manage?" There are only two reliable threshing crews hereabouts: the Larssons and the Obermanns. It would be insanity to not engage one or the other, unless a man were wealthy enough to own his own equipment and hire a team."

"We manage," said Joe.

"You're lucky then," Chip said, "to be so well off."

"We're not rich," said Josephine, who'd come up to stand beside her husband.

Chip knew that already, or he was pretty sure of it, judging by the threadbare clothing and the thin—looking back on it, some might say *gaunt*—faces of the couple.

"How *do* you get by?" Chip asked. He didn't mean to be impertinent. He was just young and curious.

"Prayer," said Joe. "We don't need money." He dropped his head so his floppy blond bangs covered up the ash marks. Sort of smiled.

Later in the week, the oldest Glodny boy told his teacher, a cousin of the Obermanns, that the family ground the wheat and had their own threshing machine. "My father made it with his own hands," he added proudly. The teacher told the ten-year-old Micah Glodny that no farmer could manage threshing on his own. Micah said that his father could and that he, Micah, was going to be there to help. The teacher responded that the law required him to be in school and he would not be excused, a comment that Micah repeated to his parents. The Glodnys, Joe and Jo, thereupon resolved to have no more dealings with town people.

No one knows how the family has survived after that, and no one was ever so ill-mannered as to inquire. But Valerie Dittmar, over at the General Emporium, recently mentioned that in the more than two years since the Ash Wednesday incident, the Poles have not purchased a stitch of clothing or provisions of any kind. Her comment prompted Greta Hanssen, whose sister-in-law's best friend is a clerk at the new federal courthouse, to let slip that not so coincidentally, mere months after Joe and Jo thumbed their noses at the whole of society, the Glodnys' wheat was taken by legal process as payment for unpaid taxes.

Greta doesn't care for gossip, but to fend off any false rumors, she filled in the details. She said even after losing a year's harvest, the Glodnys stubbornly refused to give up and planted new crops, with what resources she couldn't say. Somehow they managed. But matters came to a head a few weeks ago when federal agents attempted to oust them from the property for not paying *additional* back taxes and fines. The Glodnys, the children included, protested with all their strength and called on Jesus to defend them. Apparently the Polanders deny any government authority to tax the farm, which they claim to own by the grace of God.

With some measure of grudging respect, it's generally agreed by everybody, especially the Norwegians, that the Glodnys are in the right in this quarrel. Although, it should be said, some of the local citizenry do take issue with the Poles' claim that they obtained title to the land by a deed from Jesus Christ. Regardless, the authorities had to step in. These folks, after all, are not only different, not only poor, maybe starving, they're crazy. Brazen. They've created too much of a stir. Around here, the currency is character, and people who draw unnecessary attention to the community's furtive antigovernment political views by not paying taxes and publicly resisting liens, who don't depend on their neighbors, and who let their children go hungry are obviously lacking in some basic moral and mental foundation.

The family put up a desperate fight when the officers came for them. Constable Ness said they all seemed healthy enough, a little on the lean side for being Polish, but not sickly. And all of them plenty strong, even the young ones, ages three, eight, and twelve. The youngsters were taken to the Children's Home, where they'll be cared for until the parents are declared sane or another family member can be located. The latter is deemed unlikely, but the former is sincerely hoped for.

Fergus Falls News, *March 1907*
Polish Farmers Committed to State Mental Hospital
…For two years, these Polanders have not purchased a stitch of clothing or any groceries or any provisions of any kind. They've threshed and ground their wheat with their own threshing machine. Two years ago, their wheat was taken by legal process. They resolved to have no more dealings with town people. They lived by themselves without use of money and by the aid of prayer. They were devout Catholics and seemed to be insane on the question of religion, claiming title to land by deed from

Christ and refusing to recognize any government authority to tax or oust them from the property for nonpayment.

The family put up a desperate fight when the officers came for them. Constable Ness said they all seemed healthy enough, a little on the lean side for being Polish, but not sickly. And all of them plenty strong, even the young ones, ages five, eight, and twelve. The youngsters were taken to the Children's Home, where they'll be cared for until the parents are declared sane or another family member can be located. The latter is deemed unlikely, but the former is sincerely hoped for.

STILL HIS HOUSE

—Park Rapids, Minnesota, 2013

The husband, brain webbed by dementia, enters

the house, walks upstairs to the bedroom with

a live mouse on his shoulder. It's gray-brown,

hunched. The woman moves closer. It's not a mouse

but an orb-weaver. The husband must have

breached a garden web on his way in. Spider, she

says. The husband looks in the mirror. Spider, he

repeats. Then, slowly, he remembers and plucks

the orb-weaver from his shoulder. In this house,

still his house, no one kills a spider. To kill one in

a house brings bad luck. The husband has bad luck

already. Doesn't need more, so cupping the ticklish

creature in his hands, he carries it down the stairs,

then outside, and frees it next to the broken web.

Previously published in the Marsh Hawk Review, *Spring 2017*

CLEAN-UP MAN

In his binoculars, the man thought he saw a circling

of eagles, but I saw Minnesota turkey vultures.

Something nearby was dead. Eat or be eaten. Once in

Botswana, we watched a pride scrabbling

inside a buffalo carcass as the sated lion and his mate,

half-awake, alert for vultures or hyena, lay nearby.

This man, to his own pride known as the garbage man

or clean-up man, scavenged leftover food from all

our plates. Now appetite and senses dulled, he eats less,

has forgotten waste, dead meat, the words for vulture,

hawk, osprey. When he scans the sky with binoculars,

the only name that remains is eagle, the eagle. . . .

Previously published in PoetryBay

HUMMINGBIRDS ON THE BACKS OF GEESE

—22398 Goshawk Road

The man up north, who was putting tinted
sugar water in the hummingbird feeder, told me
hummingbirds go south every fall riding on backs
of Canada geese. The geese, those bulky yet
graceful birds who have forgotten how to migrate,
fed all winter by watered green of fairways,
soccer fields, corporate lawns, those geese whose
droppings foul the grasses. But hummingbirds, how
do they migrate without broad feathered backs to
carry them? A myth, of course. The small sprites
fly alone to Mexico where they sip fresh tropical
nectar, better by far than colored sugar water
hung outside by the same folks who think that,
up north, grass should grow green all winter.

Previously published in Great River Review, *Spring 2015*

Fiction
by Teresa Ortiz

THE CHILDREN'S MOUNTAIN

There is a mountain in the highlands of Guatemala that is inhabited exclusively by children.

This is the story Isaac told me when I first met him. I think this sounds crazy, and I don't even believe it at all. I asked him, "How do you know this? You're not even from Guatemala. You're from El Salvador." And all he said was, "I know! I've been there!"

I met Isaac at the coffee shop in south Minneapolis where I work as a barista. He was hired as the baker's assistant. We have our own oven and specialize in artisan sweet breads, and Isaac impressed everybody with his skills. He makes what he calls "*pan dulce,*" which are the sweet rolls they sell at the Mexican bakeries, except Isaac's rolls are much tastier. He told us, "That's because they're not Mexican, they are Salvadoran sweet rolls. They're better!"

Mr. Pederson was not impressed. Mr. Pederson is the head baker, and he specializes in French pastries: delicate, crumbly, buttery delicious sweets. But Isaac learned fast, and now his *pan dulce* is not only Salvadoran, it is French as well, and with this, he earned Mr. Pederson's respect. Since we added the specialty baked goods to our menu, the coffee shop fills with customers who love to complement their espresso or cappuccino with either a *croissant* or a *concha* or a *churro* or even by a crumbly *pastelito de boda*.

I also had my doubts about Isaac when I first met him. There was something weird about him. The story about the children's mountain for example. Come on! Who's going to believe that? I asked him where he learned to be such a good baker, and he said his father was a baker in El Salvador. He learned the trade from his dad growing up. That makes sense, I guess. And where did he learn to speak English? Isaac speaks fluent English with a good accent. He said he lived in a tourist area of El Salvador, where he learned English from talking to Americans. To me, that doesn't make much sense. I've never been to El Salvador, but what I've heard is that it is a very dangerous place. Why would tourists go there? I don't know. I guess once upon a time it was a tourist destination of sorts because it has beautiful beaches and volcanos. At least that's what Isaac told me. Maybe. I don't know. It could've been at one time.

*

There is a mountain in the Highlands of Guatemala that people call the children's mountain, *La Montana de los Ninos*, because only children live there.

The first time I heard about this is when I was a kid in El Salvador. I was living in El Salvador's mountain region. I lived in a small town that was beautiful and very peaceful. There was a real sense of community in my town. But then the war came to our mountain, and the army attacked us. You see, we were very independent, and the government didn't like that. After the war, the gangs took over the town. It became very dangerous for my family since my parents were members of a leftist organization in town, *la cooperativa*, where my father was a baker in the community kitchen. We fled to another area, to the coast, to a tourist town at the beach. Only my mother and kids went there. My father didn't go with us because he was well known everywhere in El Salvador. He was a member of the opposition, and it was dangerous for him. He went to the United States instead. I was fourteen years old when we moved to the coast.

It is in this town that I learned to speak English because I got a job at a small hotel, and I got to practice with the tourists there. Mostly backpackers and surfers. My work was cleaning the rooms and helping in the kitchen. My mom was a waitress at a café and bar, and she worked long hours in the day and very late into the night. I was taking care of my siblings most of the time, making sure they ate, got dressed, made it to school on time. I did this before I went to work and as soon as I came home from work. I was the oldest of four kids.

It was at this coastal town that I first heard about the children's mountain in Guatemala. People were always talking about this magical place.

*

One night when I was working late, Isaac asked me to help him with a recipe for a cranberry walnut bread that Mr. Pederson told him to bake. He asked me to help him understand what the ingredients were. I thought he had trouble with the English vocabulary, but when I read the recipe to him, it was obvious that he understood the words. That's when I realized that Isaac couldn't read. He couldn't read in English. I thought, yes, of course, why would he be able to? He learned English by talking to Americans, not by going to school.

I have a friend who teaches at an English as a Second Language school. So I recommended that Isaac enroll to work on his reading skills. He did. He was placed in the beginning-level class, which was a problem for Isaac because he is fluent in English. His classmates kept telling him he should go to the advanced class, but the teacher would not move him. You can imagine how Isaac felt. Not very good at all.

Everybody liked Isaac at the coffee shop, not only Mr. Pederson. The clients loved his pastries. They'd come into the shop and ask about the *pan dulce*. And then they'd ask for him. They'd sit there with their coffee and *pan dulce* talking to Isaac. Of course, he loved talking. He always had a story to tell them. He knew all these stories from El Salvador, legends mostly, folk tales, like one about a little guy with a big hat who comes at night and pulls your feet while you are sleeping, and one about a woman who lives underwater and appears on stormy nights. He never told the story of the children's mountain to the customers. That story he only told to me. I don't know why. The thing is, his English was always so perfect. And he was finally learning to read. Just a little bit. But learning. He said he really enjoyed school, even if he was in the beginner class. He went every night right after he finished his shift. He still asked me for help with the recipes. Sometimes he didn't understand everything.

I spent more and more time with him. I liked him. We became very close. OK. We became more than just close. I fell in love with him, and he with me. At least I think he did. With Isaac you never knew. Really.

I really don't know how this happened because, at first, I couldn't stand him. But Isaac is like that, just as he convinced Mr. Pederson to give him a job. He also won me over, and now I like him so much that I miss him when I don't see him. It was a bit weird because we were co-workers. But nobody complained. So we kept on going. We moved in together. We found a small apartment near the coffee shop. Things were really good for both of us. I could even say we were happy.

*

El Salvador is a very small country. You can't escape the violence, even if you really want to, and soon there were problems at the coast as well. Some of the kids in this town joined the gangs. They wanted to have money and power. Others were trying to leave, to make it to the United States, not because they wanted to be rich, but because they wanted to escape the gangs and the violence. I just wanted to go to the children's mountain, that is all I wanted to do. Even if my friends thought this was only a made-up story, it was my dream to go there.

One day a group of guys from one of the gangs came to the hotel where I worked. They had been demanding money from the owner, from my boss, for quite some time. He always paid. There was nothing else he could do to be left alone. He had a business to run. But things got worse. I had my own problems. I had my mom and my little brother and my two little sisters to worry about. If I lost my job, I didn't know what we would do.

The gang guys came and started shooting. I was in the lobby mopping the floor, so I was the first person to see them. They shouted at me and demanded I give them the money.

But of course I didn't have access to the money. I told them to stop shooting, that I'd call the owner. By then the tourists were all scared, running. The owner came, gave these guys the money, and he managed to get the tourists out of there. Really, the gang guys were not after them, so they let them go. They had put a pistol to my head. They told me they'd kill me. They didn't. Finally those guys left. The only good thing is that nobody got hurt. But they told me that if they saw me again, I'd be killed.

The owner closed the hotel. I lost my job, and I was afraid the gang guys would come after me next, as they had told me. I wanted to leave, but my mom decided to stay with my siblings. She said they were too little to travel to who knows where. So I left alone. This time I crossed the border into Guatemala. To be honest, I didn't know where I was going or what I was going to do when I got there. Wherever "there" was.

*

That night Isaac came home very agitated. Something had happened at his school or after school or on his way home from school. He started yelling. He was shaking. I couldn't understand him because he was mostly talking in Spanish. I asked him to explain. In English, please. He said something about a shooting, about the police, about running. The next day at work, the police came and asked for him. They said he was a witness. Only a witness of something that happened in the street. Not a person of interest. But Isaac was shaking as he talked with them. Mr. Pederson was very angry. Right away people think you are involved in something like this, even if you are only walking by. Isaac swore that he didn't have anything to do with it. But you know how it is with the police:

They always suspect you if you are brown or black, or if you don't speak perfect English.

Things got back to normal at work. We learned that this incident had nothing to do with Isaac or with his school. It was a group of people in the street who got in a fight and started shooting at each other as the students were coming out of class. The guys who did the shooting were arrested, and that was that.

Isaac decided to not go back to school. He kept talking about moving someplace else: to Saint Paul or to Richfield or to another nicer area. He kept saying that this was a dangerous neighborhood. I assured him that this was an isolated incident. I have lived in south Minneapolis all my life, and I know that sometimes things get weird, but it's not dangerous. Really. Also, we couldn't afford a better place. We had our first fight. I got so mad at Isaac that I told him he could leave if he wanted.

It was the same at work. Isaac kept screwing up. He was so distracted. Once he poured salt into the pastry mixture instead of sugar. They tasted awful. Mr. Pederson was furious. He almost fired Isaac.

*

You don't know where to go when you are a poor kid in a foreign big city. You cannot get a job because nobody will hire you. They ask you for papers that you do not have. You are alone. Where do you sleep? You have no money, not even for food.

I laid on a bench at the central park in Guatemala City. I tried to sleep. It was very cold, colder than I was used to. There was a bandstand at the park. That's when I saw them. They came out of that place under the bandstand. They were kids. Four of them. Three guys and a girl. They were about my age or younger, more like my sisters' age. I jumped up scared. I am always thinking of the gang guys. I am always afraid. They came up closer to me. Started talking, asking questions of me. They wanted to know why I was sleeping there. They were acting as if this were their home and I was an intruder. I told them I had no place to go. Colocho, Catracho, Bayron, and La Wendy. Those were their names. They lived there. They slept under the bandstand. Always running from the police. But they are not gang guys. It is just that they don't have a home to live in, and the police don't like them, they said, because they are dirty, because they sleep on the street.

It was not only them; I met a lot of kids who also lived in the city streets. They were always running away from the police. One of their friends had been killed by the police. Others were in juvenile jail. Some of them were used by the gangs to sell drugs.

I stayed there with them for about two weeks. Not a place that I liked. I missed El Salvador. I missed my small town in the mountains, the smell of fresh bread from my dad's bakery, my job at the coast, my mom, and my siblings. I missed home. But I didn't miss the gangs, and with these kids, I felt safe.

Once I even asked them about the children's mountain. Catracho started to laugh. "Everybody in Guatemala knows about the mountain," he said. He called it "the mountain," as if there were only one in the entire country. "But seriously now. Everybody knows that this is just a story. Not real. It doesn't exist. It is just like 'El Sombreron.' Just a story, man. Just made-up legend. If it was real, we would all be there."

I left after two weeks. I had to get going.

*

Isaac did not come home. He didn't come to work either. He just disappeared. He left. We had another fight the night before. This was even worse than the first one. He had been screwing up at work. Mr. Pederson had lost complete confidence in him. I told him to watch it, that he'd lose his job if he went on like that. He started yelling. As usual, when he's really mad, he yelled in Spanish, and of course it makes things worse because I didn't understand him, so I start yelling too.

He stormed out of the house, slamming the door. This was two weeks ago, and he hasn't returned. I'm worried that something bad has happened to him. I worry that he's been hurt or was deported or something. I don't know what. I'm worried.

*

After I left Guatemala City, I traveled all over the country, asking here and there how to get to where I wanted to go. Nobody knew. Nobody could tell me. I was guided merely by my instincts and by the stories I had heard before. This happened almost twenty years ago, when the millennia was still new. I was only sixteen years old.

I made it all the way to the rainforest by hitching rides from tourists and locals alike. When I got to the end of the road, I started to walk. As I walked deeper into the jungle, I was surrounded by vegetation, I was immersed in a sea of forest, so many strange plants of so many shapes and colors that I had never seen. The forest was so thick around me that I had to keep cutting the brush with the machete Bayron gave me. I went on cutting at every other step to move from one place to the next.

As I walked up hill toward the mountains, the vegetation subsided. Just a bit. But the clouds moved in, and the rain started to fall hard like a thick curtain. I walked up hill for days in that cold, drizzly rain. I was soaked. The mud was so deep under me that it came all the way to my knees. It was difficult to walk. Around me it was all dark. But in spite of the mud, I recognized the feeling of a path under my feet, a path formed by many other feet that had stepped on it before me, a path that hopefully would take me to the top of the mountain. I kept walking, moving between the trees, among the brush, following that path that I could barely see. I was cold and wet and hungry and so tired. Everything hurt in my body. I climbed that hill all night until the light changed and I recognized that it was daytime. The fog was still so thick that I could not see where I was going. I looked up and saw that the clouds were covering the mountains, the earth, everything.

That is when I began to hear a distant sound; it was like birds singing, like animals running. I heard the distant singing in a language I did not understand. It was not Spanish. It was not English. It was like angels. I heard the drumming to the rhythm of my own steps as I continued to climb up, for hours. And then the fog burned off, and the sun came out. That's when I saw it.

I stood there transfixed, my legs stuck in the mud, shaking, my body drenched in sweat and rain, my eyes covered with raindrops and tears, which made it difficult to really take a good look. It was as if the stars had fallen down to earth, and they were dancing rhythmically toward me. It was as if the moon up in the sky were pulling the thousands of dancing stars with a string. Marching to the rhythm of the drums. I heard them singing. Chanting. Hundreds of marchers with torches in their hands, they looked as if they were stars rolling downhill.

But they were not stars, they were not angels. They were real, human, living kids, singing with the ancient voices of the mountains, with the voices of their ancestors, our ancestors, those voices that in the city only hide, but here, in the jungle, they come alive. They sing with power, sounding like angels. Downhill, directly in front of me, were hundreds of other kids, living kids, drumming as loud and as happily as if they were in a rock concert. But this was no rock concert.

This was like heaven.

A SLOW MOVING NIGHT

On the high, mountainous land of the Sanaag region in Somalia, *jiilaal* season showed neither compassion nor mercy on its inhabitants. The trees stood still, the boughs refused to sway, even slightly, and the reflection of the sun's rays shone on rocks with flat surfaces.

A herd of sheep and goats moved about in mad fury trying to seek sanctuary under the shade of a tree, which had shrunk within the past two hours or so from a sizable length able to provide shelter to a negligible hue. Once they got under the tree and into the shade, the sheep huddled in concert. Some sat, some remained standing, and some hid their heads under the others. But the goats butted one another, competing for better positions. The day progressed slowly beyond the zenith, yet the heat persisted, driving the herd to a delirious lust for water.

One ewe finally had enough. Suddenly she broke out of the herd's temporary huddle and moved on, westward. One by one, the rest of her family flocked behind. The goats, too, left the shade but, instead of trailing the sheep, chose to scatter about, scrub grazing.

Thousands of years of experience, passed down from generation to generation, had taught herdsmen to recognize the behaviors of certain animals. Thus it was quite apparent to both my brother and me that the sheep were in search of water. It was my job and his, however, to keep them away from drinking, regardless. The reasons were many, but chief among them was that, in the dry *jiilaal* season as well as the *xagaa*, nomads in Somalia water-feed their livestock in a managed manner. We are able to weigh the severity of drought by estimating how much moisture the trees have stored in their roots and how much juice is left in their leaves. The data we gather help us decide how long a flock of sheep or goats can lust for water but continue to survive without it. It's a matter of economic grazing, calculated by the amount of available food. Trying to control the amount of water our animals are taking in, we make sure there is enough space left in their stomachs for fodder as well.

Naturally, sheep are a bit slower and less adventurous than goats. Feeling safer in packs, they neither spread over nor ascend to the highest peaks of mountains. Goats, on the other hand, climb high on the roughest rocks, graze precariously on tilted slopes and cliff edges. Yet always alert, they rarely let a foe catch them off guard. If they ever stumble into a mishap and awaken a beast stealing a nap, they let out a high-pitched distress bleat. The sheep, however, may feast on foliage even while a coyote is goring them. And just in case you might ask, sheep baa mainly on two occasions: one, when they are looking for their broods and two, when they are in search of water. Yet both goats and sheep share a single misfortune: the need for a

vigilant, tireless watcher, necessitated by a plethora of predators (hyenas, leopards, jackals, coyotes, lions, cheetahs, and
men).

For his size and age, it was not an accident that my brother
instinctively saw fit to follow the breakaway herd of sheep, for
he knew that I, the older of the two of us and thus the stronger,
was going to make him do so anyway. I would try my best to
avoid sweating more than he.

From far off, the howling of baboons echoed through the
valley beds. And to the west, a falcon soared so high in the
heavens, I wondered whether it was searching for a long-lost
companion or was just cheerfully flying for the joy of it.

My train of thought was rudely interrupted by an army of
ants approaching only inches away. I faced them as though
they were an invading enemy and sized them up. I was rather
disarmed by their ingenuity to serve the full circle of life. Some
carried cut-away green leaves ten times heavier than their own
weight; others carried burdens weighing as much as themselves; yet some simply followed the rest in droves. I tried to
trace back to their origin but saw only a tiny, dark line snaking
through the terrain.

As I followed the trail, I saw a chameleon lashing a vindic-
tive tongue, tossing ants into his mouth and gobbling them
down. He barely acknowledged me before scurrying off. I
rushed forward to survey the damage he had inflicted on the
delicate, almost invisible path.

The line was battered in several places. So a lonely ant, trying to go about her daily chores, appeared confused, stopped,
ran, stopped, and ran again. Another befuddled one ran back
and forth, then left and right. Yet another, carrying a cut-away
clump of leaves, veered off to the left, following an invisible
map. Then a lonely one emerged from the dust and continued

imperviously, as though determined to lead them all away. Alas, not a single ant followed. They no longer marched with carefree pride and seemed to have lost that sense of marveling at the natural beauty around them.

Of course, I thought a human being should mend the mess, so I lay tiny twigs where I thought the line was broken on one end all the way to the other end where I thought it had begun. Then I picked a twig and placed it in front of the disoriented ants. When an ant got on it, I transferred it to the line I had created with twigs. But each one declined to follow the line.

"Let them doom themselves to their stupid death," I consoled myself. "God helps those who help themselves."

Not more than a minute had passed when, to my dismay, two ants emerged from each end of the line, met in the middle, kiss-greeted, and then proceeded on their respective ways. In another minute, columns miraculously converged from opposing ends of an invisible line. A parade began on a single thread, with all now facing the same direction, as though nothing had disturbed the path.

I was about to leave when I saw another group from the same colony drag a small dead gecko with a precision that human soldiers would have difficulty matching. The unfortunate creature was turned over, her white belly blue where multiple ant bites had injected poison into her bloodstream.

The army, many under the tiny gecko, latched on to the legs, transporting an eliminated foe.

The ants' ingenious, collaborative effort engaged my curiosity until the distinctive bleat of a distraught goat caught me off guard. And then it hit me. I had committed the cardinal sin that all herdsmen must avoid: You should never let your herd out of your sight. As I dashed off in the direction of the goat's plea, I heard my brother cry out from the middle of the valley bed. I knew immediately that he had fallen off the edge of a steep slope somewhere. Ignoring the cries of the bleating goat, I took off to find him.

Frantically I ran down the slope, dislodging shells, stones, sticks and all. The cacophony of the tiny avalanche echoed throughout the valley below, causing the goats to stampede and climb to the highest tip of the other side of the ridge. Heading down in a haze of confusion, I came upon Shamad, my favorite goat, who had just delivered twin kids. I could see from a distance that one of the kids was waddling, the placenta still swathed to him. I predicted a problem: that this could attract the most heinous, hideous creature of all, the spotted hyena. But I had no time to attend to them. The fear that I was going to find my brother with lacerations and broken bones besieged me. "God, please don't let it be the spinal cord," I pleaded over and over again.

My legs were about to give out. And now as I charged through the thorny underbrush, my shabby clothes were torn to pieces. But I kept on pleading with God to give my brother a chance and not penalize him for my witless neglect. I solemnly swore that if he would heed my plea today, I would never, ever again be consumed with admiration and awe of those small creatures that had rendered me mindless.

I was, as well, leery of how I was going to convince my mother later on that whatever calamity had befallen our goats happened because of "God's will." She was a severe disciplinarian and, worse, had already admonished me on numerous occasions to be vigilant to avoid all possible mishaps. I knew she was going to wail at me and bemoan my carelessness.

I began to pray for a mild beating or, better yet, a harsh scolding.

All of these thoughts collided in my head as I hurtled down the steep slope. Fears for my own survival were interrupted by the cries from the sheep and my brother's piercing howls.

And then I spotted him! It looked like he was just sitting on the ground, but as I came closer, I saw that he had a sheep by the leg and was pulling it away from something. When I was a few feet away, I realized he was in a contentious tug of war with one of the most dangerous predators, the leopard. The elusive beast had strangled a thoroughbred ram and torn a slab of fresh flesh from its jowl. Blood was trickling from the wound to the ground. The leopard, crouching, looked ready to pounce. Every time my brother tried to pull the ram away, the leopard, claws fully extended, feinted to lunge but hung on with his powerful jaws. Whenever the leopard made his deceptive move, my brother would let go of the leg, jump back, and wail louder. Startled, the leopard would recoil, growling, and my brother would summon the courage to grab the leg again.

My heart froze with fear as my brother looked back at me. Not knowing how I could save him, I ducked down. My petulant brother, however, was putting up a valiant fight and expected to be bailed out or, at least, assisted.

It should not surprise you that I wanted to do just that, but could not wrench the tiniest bit of courage from my soul. Supporting my weight with one hand, I freed the other for defense and raised my head from behind a bush. There was the leopard in full view. His sheer bulk forced me to wish that my brother would not play this game. I wondered what he was trying to prove and how on earth he was going to get out of this stalemate.

Eyes bulging, my brother looked into the brush, as though that would hasten help. The leopard rose slightly, seized the ram with his claws, and tried to snatch it away. I quickly ducked down again, praying that the leopard had not spotted me.

By now the silent ram had had enough of the pain. He baaed so loudly that the rest of his family, huddled only a few feet away, felt compelled to join his plea. Contributing to the chorus of terror, my brother shrieked like a soul under siege. I yearned for the land to give way under me and begged God to deposit me back into my mother's warm womb.

"Doogle, where are you?" my brother called.

Let me tell you, I was not impressed at all that Taahe had thrown my name into the ethereal air when all he had to do was let go of the ram. We had plenty of sheep, and losing one, even a thoroughbred ram, wasn't going to make us poorer.

But Taahe continued to call me. "Doogle, show me your bravery, show me the valor you mustered when you fought off that jackal long ago!"

What my brother could not remember, because I had never told a soul, was how terrified I had been facing the jackal he was referring to.

Hearing my name disseminated so generously into the air, I decided to come out to defend it. Yet it dawned on me that my brother was not fair, for he was inveigling me to face the "dean of danger." This was not a jackal, and he knew it.

He kept the heat on, furiously fanning it. "Brother Doogle," he yelled. "The whole neighborhood knows you are brave. I know you are brave, and the leopard knows you are brave. That's why I've been waiting for you, so when he feels your aura of gallantry approaching, he will unlock his jaws, rein in his claws, and slouch away!"

I was ashen with fear and anger. Surely the predator was going to take up his offer to challenge me at any moment now.

Yet I wanted my brother to believe in me, and I wanted him to keep calling me brave. And if you ask, yes, I enjoyed it while it lasted. What I was objecting to, nevertheless, was calling me brave only if I confronted the leopard! Why could one still not be called brave if he chose a nonconfrontational approach?

I was not going to show my face because I knew this majestic creature would cast his spell on me and I would cave in, probably whimpering with fear. I also knew that my family would scold me, that if I let the leopard have this ram for a meal, he would come back for another and another and another...

I did not want to let my brother believe that I was not worthy of his praise, but still I could not move a muscle when, again, he called, "Brother Doogle, this fool leopard has not yet gotten a whiff of you. Please hurry. Just come closer, and he will vanish in fear from your mere presence." My brother always spoke with the maturity of unmatched eloquence.

I, on the other hand, the one who was devoid of wisdom, thought, *No, little man, no. This is a leopard, the most resourceful, elusive cat of all. Once I come out of hiding, he will cast his spell on me and leave the ram to feast on me.*

I forced myself to crouch on all fours, as though I were about to take off at full speed. But my legs were wobbling, my hands were weak, my heart was pounding like a bouncing ball. I grabbed my spineless soul and attempted to stand upright. I was not fully erect when I began to backpedal, hoping to hide myself in the shadowed field for a moment, before galloping away at full speed.

Alas, my brother turned around and caught me in my compromising crouch. In that instant, he changed. He stopped chanting my praises and began to chide. "You coward," he barked. "Where the hell are you trying to run off to?"

Furious, I stood up and, chin high, tossed up some phony courage. My brother was holding the ram by the leg while the leopard still clutched the shoulders, but once he began to shout at me, he loosened his grip. The leopard seized the moment to snatch the meal away.

Completely letting go of the leg, my brother dashed over and pasted himself onto me so tightly that I thought a spirit had possessed him. I let him cling to me, thankful that he had let the ominous enemy loose.

In relief, my body let go. Sadly, I wet my pants just when my brother harnessed himself onto me, right after the leopard plunged his fangs into the ram's throat.

The poor ram had been instantly overpowered and was not able to manage even a minor, convulsing move. He shivered a few feeble twitches. It was all over.

In earnest, the killer began to tend his prey, letting go of the throat, licking the blood oozing from gashes where his fangs had penetrated, growling at us every now and then. He straddled the carcass, grasped its neck in his jaws, lifted it up, and sidle-dragged the body away—all the while keeping an eye on us. Growling and dragging the body, he lumbered up the steep slope, behind the thick brush, beside the huge rock that seemed as if it would roll away if touched, past the dry weeds, and onto the top of the slope where he disappeared.

Taahe released me from his clutch and let out a sigh. He took a few steps away and started to examine me. He stopped short as he became aware of his own strange discomfort.

"Doogle," he started, looking at his pants, first one leg, then the other, then at his palms, then twisting his pants from front to back. "What—?"

"What's the matter, Taahe?" I interrupted, feeling timid.

"Do you notice that I am wet?" he asked. And to my dismay, he began to get closer, examining me with a look of disgust and surprise.

"What are you talking about?" I cried, mimicking his conspiratorial gaze.

"Why am I wet?" he asked.

I wanted to come up with an ingenious way to protest my innocence by denying that I had wet my pants when fear had penetrated my total being and I could no longer will my internal organs to obey me.

"I had my period," I said off-handedly.

My brother jumped five feet away, laughing hysterically. "Since when did men begin to menstruate?" he barked.

"Since Adam and Eve," I persisted. "Besides, what the hell do you know about men's menstruation? You are too young to know and too inexperienced to care."

"Unlike you, at least I have been around long enough to know that our dad has never menstruated." My brother jabbed me.

"How on earth do you know that? And let me hear you clearly—are you accusing me of cowardice when I just saved your ass?"

My brother was not ready for confrontation, I guess, or perhaps he realized how desperate I had become to defend my deflated ego.

"I am only saying that I have never heard Dad or Mom or anyone else talk about this, Doogle," he said.

"I'll have you know," I said, "that women have theirs and men have theirs too. But the man type of menstruation is different from women's."

I thought I had convinced him when my brother asked, "And Doogle, where does this type come out?"

Damn it, I thought. What the hell, I was going to say that men fart theirs when they are scared, but at that moment a throng of sheep that had been huddling under the trees, hugging the waterhole, suddenly stampeded toward us. I jumped up and took off, saved from any further discussion on a topic that had gotten way out of hand. My brother was not far behind.

We soon collected the rest of the herd, goaded them out of the waterhole, and moved them up the steep climb to the top of the mountain. Taahe had not exchanged a word with me on our way up. On top of the ridge where we would be able to see any enemy approaching but surrounded by steep cliffs, populated by precariously perched boulders and atrophied trees that were lean and gnarled, we let the herd graze.

Abruptly, again, we heard Shamad bleating. My favorite goat with the twin kids that I had stumbled upon earlier and then temporarily forgotten was still in danger.

I pelted away in horror, sprinting to reach her. Because of my knowledge of how jackals exercised their primal cruelty on many a goat, I thought I might be able to save her. Racing to reach my destination, it hit me that the rest of the herd of goats was nowhere in sight. Regret rose in a wave of nausea. Shamad was not just a goat. She was my treasure. She was blessed with a wealth of milk, was very friendly, and whenever I called her in the middle of the night from the corral, she would rush to reach me, while the remaining rascal goats would wait for me to sludge through their manure to get to them.

I raced from the top of the ridge, down the twisting slope to the riverbed, and up the opposite slope. With aching muscles and panting breath, I pushed forward. I could hear the rest of the goat herd in the distance, but, ignoring them, I used my remaining strength to get to Shamad. There she was, oblivious to the dangers around her, caring for nothing but her new kids.

The kids were not strong enough to follow their mother yet, so I would have to carry them. I picked them up by the paws, hung them over my arms, and began to make my way down the slope, through the valleybed, and up the other side of the ridge. Shamad was right on my heels, bleating as she tagged along. I was exhausted, and every few yards I would stop, put down the kids, sit for a minute to catch my breath, and then, lifting them up again, trudge a few more yards. I knew I had no time to waste to catch up with Taahe, where I would leave the kids and Shamad, before setting off in search of the rest of the goat herd. If I let dusk arrive without the herd secured in their corral, the animal kingdom of carnivores would feast on them.

When I did not immediately find my brother and his herd of sheep, I began to fear another mishap. Trickling sweat, kids draped over each arm, and Shamad trailing behind me, I negotiated the treacherous slope.

Then I spied Taahe. Thankfully, he had already collected the sheep and was in the process of prodding them back home. As he approached me with an appearance of manufactured menace, I knew he was going to remind me that, as head of the herdsmen, I had failed in my duty. He would not let me forget that I had committed the cardinal sin of losing half of my flock.

Until that moment, I had entertained a vacuous hope that my pride would remain intact. Now it was quite apparent there was precious little I could do but come to terms with my embarrassment. A chill rushed up my spine.

In the dry season particularly, goats are highly valued for their enviable ability to provide milk. Thus a failure to find them was not only going to be unbearably embarrassing but economically devastating.

The sun was hanging low and seemed to be racing to rest behind the imposing mountain in the west. We both knew what that meant: no time to recover the remaining members of the herd. The legacy of a disastrous day in history was looming. Whatever manhood was left in me was riding on a boat of despair, so I was desperate to find the appropriate words and at least feign a recovery attempt.

"So," he said. "That's it, I guess. I mean, what else is there to do? The sun is about to descend. The goats are nowhere around, and every bastard predator is going to be on the prowl in a few…."

"Shut up," I shouted. "Shut up."

He bent down, picked up several pebbles, and randomly threw them one after the other. Then he turned to me with a look that said "get the hell out of my sight," but instead he said, "Why don't you try to see whether you can find them? Goats are very smart. They can outmaneuver most predators, perching on peaks where no danger can molest them. Or they might just choose to head on home, and in that case, they'll meet you halfway."

He had now infused me with a bit of hope that if only I could gather the courage to go, I might meet the herd midway. I could at least show some effort.

"Taahe, you're right," I said. "I have to go and search. Take the sheep home, but whatever you do, do not let our mother know about me and the missing goats!"

Taahe was not amused. "You're putting yourself in danger," he yelled. "We've already lost half of what we are worth. We are on the verge of getting into the neighborhood, the gossip gale, and you're asking me not to tell! I could try not to say a word, but how will that be possible?"

"Please, I beg you," I pleaded. "You know, I'm going to find them and bring them home. All of them!"

My brother shook his head in disgust, picked up the two kids, one in each arm, and walked away toward the sheep. Shamad, who had never before wavered in her loyalty to me, chose to trail him. Taahe moved from one wing of the sheep herd to the other, gathering them into a throng and then goading them toward home.

I waited a while to see whether he might change his mind, to come back and collect me, but to no avail. Of course he had caught me in a violation of the herdsmen's golden law and, at the same time, recognized that dusk was ominously approaching with its menacing darkness. He was not willing to wade through the danger or wage a war with complacency. Thus he moved on, decisive.

Watching my little brother turn on his heels made me mad but forced me not to waste a precious minute. I took off and ran with such speed that I didn't notice the thorns ripping through the flesh of my legs, leaving wounded streaks on my calves and thighs. Racing from the top of the ridge, descending into the valley, and then climbing again, I finally reached the peak where I thought I had last heard the goats' bleats. But to my despair, not a single goat showed herself in appreciation of my valiant attempt. The silent solitude severed my serenity, so I moved about, restless, climbing one rock after another, scaling a thousand-year-old tree to extend my range of view. Nothing. Nothing gave me the slightest glimmer of hope. I looked to the west, and my heart sank. The sun was receding behind a hollow mountain that cast its gloomy shadow.

I hollered at the sun to slow her descent. She ignored my pleas.

With nowhere to go and nothing else to do, I chose to stay in the thousand-year-old acacia tree. I crawled up and perched on the base of a branch that was high out of the hoodlum hyena's reach. Watching the sun's lazy descent, my heart sank. Thick darkness fell, closing in around me. I found solace in knowing that lions were not going to maul me tonight. Lions had no ecological attachment to this high mountainous land; hyenas were too heavy to heave themselves up into my tree; human thieves were too impatient to take any interest; cheetahs were too timid to tussle with me; and jackals were too clever to waste tactical maneuvers on me. But still, the daring leopard could dispatch her demons of death.

I wrestled with what to do if disaster came. Solutions evaded me. The blanket of darkness, the howling of the jackals, the baboons that began to yowl, and the batches upon batches of bugs that bit my skin, all kept me paralyzed.

Sometime that evening, I heard my mother calling my name, "Doogle! Doogle!"

Every inch of my body was immobilized, even my voice box. I was terrified predators would hear me if I called and have me for a meal.

Her voice reverberated throughout the hollow valley. She called all night long, alternating the pitch of her voice from high to low. All I could do was muster the strength to keep myself in the tree, neither falling asleep nor muttering a word. As I heard my mother mourn, night washed me with dew. It was a merciless, slow-moving night. But, as she probably intended, her distant cries kept me company, hopeful that the dawn would provide a safe return home.

Throughout the night, I suffered the savage beating of hysteria until finally daybreak dispatched the hopes that had departed with the darkness. An orange glow radiated sages of amber beauty that I had known and seen so often but never admired. Resuscitated by the sun's morning rays, my fear vanished. Within an hour of those first morning rays, I felt warmer and wiser.

The limbs that were numb last night, the larynx that lacked the courage to cough, and the legs that were limp miraculously filled with renewed vigor, and I climbed down. Once I landed on the ground, I hastened to take an inventory, checking to see whether the host tree had taken any of me for itself. Satisfied that I was whole, I hurried to my mother. Suddenly I heard her melodic voice again and melted into exuberant waves of emotional exhilaration. As soon as I saw her, I dashed forward with maddening speed and threw myself into her arms, holding on to her ever-so tightly, weeping.

It seemed ages before we both gained our composure. She released me from her embrace, held me back to stare lovingly at me before pulling me back into her again. She did that many times, as though she were not convinced it was me.

"I thought I had lost you last night," she finally uttered in a hoarse voice. "Hooyo, don't ever, ever do that to me again."

"Yes, Hooyo," I responded.

"No matter what, do you hear me, Hooyo?" she asked.

"Yes, Hooyo, I will never do that again."

"Whatever else is in danger, I don't care, Hooyo. Your life is more important to me than everything we have. Do you hear me, Hooyo?" my mother repeated, wiping the tears from my face with the hem of her gown.

"Yes, Hooyo." For the first time, I savored the meaning and weight of the word *hooyo*, which means mother or my child, thus used interchangeably in Somali.

"Now, let's find those useless goats that have caused me so much grief and almost cost me my son's life. OK?"

"Yes, Hooyo," I said, surprised that she was no longer distraught nor distressed about the loss of the "precious" goats whose care she had always grumbled about.

"Where were they when you saw them last? And where the hell were you anyway?"

O, ooh, she cha-a-anged her mind, watch out, I thought.

But she checked herself. "Never mind about where you were. Just tell me where you last saw them."

Over the mountaintop, then over another and another, we finally came upon a gigantic rise fortified by cliffs and flanked by chasms. These cliffs and chasms were empowered by solid, massive rocks seated in the corners of each twist of the trail. Carved by nature, in the middle of the mountain face, was a dark cave normally inhabited by baboons and not easily accessible to the hated hyena. However, it was not a safe haven from cheetahs, jackals, man, or that most ingenious cat—the leopard.

There they were, our throng of goats, chewing their cud. My mother approached, slow and cautious, as though she were invading a herd of wild gazelles. She called a few goats by their names, and they responded with a friendly bleat. We waded through the flock, petting each goat in passing to show our gratitude for the reunion.

They rose and began to mill about. My mother grabbed one of the strongest he-goats by the leg, but he jumped and jerked away. Getting ahold of him by the ear, she hauled him out of the cave. He leaped into the air, landed on all fours, and dashed down the slope before halting abruptly. He appeared to give a silent signal to the rest of the herd. In a minute, they followed by twos, threes, and on and on until my mother, who was trying to make a head count, decided to restrict the flow.

"Ninety-eight, ninety-nine, hundred, hundred one…"

I had no clue when or how she had reached the hundreds.

"…Hundred two, three, hundred four,…hundred seven, hundred eight."

"Did I say hundred five and six?" she asked.

"Yes, Hooyo," I said, trying not to contradict her.

"Hundred ten, hundred eleven, hundred twelve," she went on, looking back, then letting some pass by.

"Hundred thirty-seven, hundred-thirty-eight, nine. Ooh, they are all here, thank God for His mercy." She signed as the last two goats scuttled past her.

"Or did I overcount them?" she whispered to herself.

"No, no," she reassured herself. "It doesn't matter much now even if there are one or two or twenty missing. I have my son and, if not all, most of my prized goats. Thank God."

She dropped her stick and opened her arms up for me, smiling ever so gently. She clutched me so tight around the ribcage that I had to beg her to go easy. Minutes passed before she seemed satisfied. She let go, stood back, held my hand, twirled me about, pulled me to herself, held me away, then inspected me all over again before she led me out of the cave into the herd.

"Now," she ordered. "Collect them from the left, and let's get home before the children let the sheep out of the corral." She presented me with her herding stick before walking to the other side of the herd.

"*Jii, jii, jii, hoow, hoow, hoow, caa, caa,*" she howled, ordering the herd to stay tightly together as she guided them back home.

On the way back, the sky turned to azure. The eerie feeling of desolation had departed. The sound of the goats' hooves beating on the poor earth resounded like that of pouring rain. A mile or so away from our enclosure, a pack of the most despised creatures of the savannah, the hyenas, appeared in our view. We, the mother-son pair of brave souls, broke down with laughter, for we were aware of how ridiculous the hyenas looked. They had lost their opportunity to feast on our herd.

"If only they had known where to look," my mother quipped. "If only they had known where to look last night."

I laughed with exaggerated disgust at the hyenas' misfortune.

Yards from our enclosure, the rest of the family—sisters, brother Taahe, all—came out to greet us.

Taahe rushed toward me with an embellished pace, then suddenly halted a few feet away.

"Has your men's menstruation let up?" he called out for all to hear, laughing. Then he dashed away, pairing up with Mom, and from behind her, waving at me furtively.

Previously published in Ahmed Yusuf's collection, The Lion's Binding Oath and Other Stories, *Catalyst Press, June 19, 2018*

THE KITCHEN IN THE CINDERBLOCK HOUSE

It was late fall, the sky darkening and the air cold, when our parents drove us up to the house we would be living in from now on. My brothers, Pete and Matt, were first- and second-graders, and I had just turned four when we moved. Following Dad, we walked through an opening in the lilac hedge that hid the house and yard from the street. The hedge, dense as a thicket of briars, veiled four large stone pillars that stood like sentries along the verge of the street. There was already snow on the ground. Dad called it a blanket of snow, so we thought it would be warm. Holding me back, Dad laughed as the boys threw themselves into the snow and howled with surprise. Mother came up the sidewalk carrying a small suitcase and told the boys to be careful walking, snow was slippery.

"Let's get the kids in the house, Gene," she said. "It's cold."

Looking up at the house, it seemed like we had entered a different world. The high, square cinderblock house loomed large and gray. With its half-walled front porch, the house seemed to belong to a dark fairy tale. Its only ornament was the silhouette of a large swan attached to the front screen door. This did not resemble the beautiful, big house that Dad had described so enthusiastically. It was too dark out to see the crowning glory of the house: the lake behind it. And it didn't matter now; it was dark, freezing over, covered with snow. What a different world this was from our home in Vacaville: none of the warmth, sun, friends, and familiarity of the small California house we had always lived in.

We had left California weeks or months ago. I don't know how many days it took to drive across the country, Mother and Dad telling stories, leading us in sing-alongs of the old standard car songs, playing I-spy games, arguing. I drifted and squirmed with boredom, unaware of time, looking for animals—especially horses—along the way. I looked as close as I could when large animals appeared for those special ones who were my familiars. There were two shape-shifters in every herd that I could tell were animated by a spirit; always the two most beautiful (black or the deepest brown) who knew me; they watched for me. They became secret friends, keeping pace with the car, always ahead and waiting for me as we passed a farm or ranch. They were accompanying me, befriending me on the long journey.

The kitchen in that old house was made strange and wonderful by nooks and doorways and dark passageways leading in and out of it. The three of us kids rarely tired from running around the house, up and down and through these passageways. Mother disapproved of this. We were likely to do harm at every turn. From the kitchen we ran into the narrow corridor that passed tall buffets in the butler's pantry (A butler's pantry? We gasped at the idea.), then released us into the dining room. In the pantry, glasses and dishes were stacked for dinner.

"Don't run through the pantry. You'll knock off those dishes!"

Out of the pantry, we turned right and gained speed sailing through the high-ceilinged dining and living rooms. They had scratched wood floors and heavy white-painted trim in the style of the turn of the last century.

"Don't slide on those floors in your stocking feet! You'll get splinters!"

After negotiating the corner and sweeping into the broad, open living room, we came to traverse the most unusual stairs we had ever seen, stairs that slowed us down. Wide steps from the living room led up to a landing. From there we chose which way to go. If we turned right, we'd go up a steep flight of stairs to the four bedrooms above. In a different game, scarier than this one, played after dark, we would turn right to go up the stairs. My brothers made up stories about the ghost in the house, and one by one we would each run into all the upstairs rooms, touch something special in each one, and run back down the stairs. We counted the seconds to see how fast each child could do it and declared a winner.

Rather, in this game, our running-around-the-house game, we turned left at the stair landing to descend the narrow steps that ran into the closed door leading back to the kitchen. This required slowing down. Each one of us, as we came through, would need to lean down, reach for the doorknob, open the door carefully, check the kitchen for Mother, and close the door again. My brothers would race. I was not expected to keep up; if they passed me twice, I would be out, still too little to play.

"Don't slam that door. Don't run through here. I'm working!" she'd yell with a swipe at us with a spatula or whatever utensil was in hand. She was so easily irritated in this house. In

California, she had been such a fun, happy mother. We also had changed, had newfound power: We were bigger, smarter, had seen so much of the world crossing the country. In this house, there were so many opportunities to stir up mischief.

Mother's parents, Grandma Annie and Grandpa Gus, drove from a small town in central Wisconsin more than once that first fall and winter to help. We were always excited when they came and ran into their arms. Grandpa arrived with jelly beans in his pocket, sneaking some into our hands when he hugged us, telling us, "Hide them, it's a secret."

"Dad! You'll spoil those kids' appetites. I've got supper ready," Mother would complain. He'd laugh and scold her for being too strict. "All kids need treats," he'd pronounce. By the next day, Grandma Annie would already be in charge. The house needed a thorough cleaning. The kids needed looking after. Grandma and Mother grumbled about the state of the house, but Mother needed to rest. As Grandma went about the cleaning, she put the three of us kids to work.

"Idle hands are the devil's workshop." Grandma was fond of old sayings, silly rhymes and verses that she quoted to instruct or entertain. There was no use trying to dodge her. Sweet as a grandmother could be, she didn't tolerate shirkers.

"Come in here and help," she'd cajole the nearest child, "and it'll be done in two shakes of a lamb's tail." We were drawn to her side, and as we worked, she would tell stories of growing up on the prairie in North Dakota with her good-for-nothing brothers and the native people who lived nearby.

Grandma seemed always to be making something wonderful at the old-fashioned stove that was tucked into an alcove opposite the rest of the kitchen. The back burner of the stove was covered with a black iron plate fitted with a curved handle for lifting. Underneath that plate was a well that held a big kettle. Grandma would heat up cooking oil in that kettle and drop in round rings of doughnut batter that would soon be dancing. She rarely did anything that did not require a child's hand. I sprinkled cinnamon and sugar on them while they were hot.

Later, I learned that Grandma and Grandpa made the long drive from Nekoosa because they were worried about Alice, our mother. She had been in the hospital for a long time the summer before in California. We children knew that. We did not know that she had had a radical mastectomy and large doses of radiation. Even when we saw her scars and dismemberment, the skin graft and the large, pale rectangle on her thigh where skin was taken, none of us knew what that meant or remember being aware that anything was out of the ordinary. We remember Mrs. Day, who stayed with us, taking care of us for a while. I think she slept in the house with us for a period of time. Was it days? Or weeks?

When Mother came home from the hospital, we thought her illness was over and done. Surely all women came home from the hospital looking like she did. Those times were different; adults did not discuss what was going on with children. We only knew that the family was going to move away to Minnesota. Dad had gotten a new job at the Honeywell headquarters in Minneapolis, and we would be closer to Mother's family. Trying to win me over, Dad painted pictures describing the beauty of Minnesota and its lakes.

"I'm going to find us a big house on a lake, Mary! You'll love the lake. And swimming! You'll be swimming like a little fish."

Dad loved it when he could get me to jump into a swimming pool and paddle toward him. Even though I was always afraid, I always succumbed to his coaxing and jumped. He would pull me out of the water as I sank and praise me for how I swam. But I did not believe that I would love this new place he talked about, or that moving away would be a good thing. I was nearly old enough to join the gang of kids—the Saltzmans, Jeannie Norris, Augie Marino—who ran from yard to yard playing with cap guns and jump ropes and softballs. I was almost old enough to be free from a mother's supervision. I would lose all that if we moved now. I would lose my rightful place with this longed-for tribe.

"And you'll get to see Grandma and Grandpa lots more too," he told Matt and Pete and me. We heard not a grace note of worry in his voice. Nor did we hear that Mother's family might be needed in case things did not go well.

*

My brothers went to school the week after our move to Forest Lake. Matt had always performed well in school and been quick to make friends, but here he was strangely quiet and struggled at first to fit in. His teacher found him sitting up against the school wall during recess, coloring little stones. Pete, generally uncontrollable, naturally created chaos in the classroom. He loved his first-grade teacher, Mrs. Nelson. The worse his behavior during the day, the greater his love for her at its end. He was known to take her hand at the end of a school day and kiss it.

"Thank you, Mrs. Nelson, for a wonderful day!"

When we lived in Vacaville, Pete and I had once schemed to trade places. There, he had hated school and planned an escape from kindergarten at recess; this would be my opportunity to sneak in and sit in his seat. No one would notice. He explained how to find his desk at the back of the room. We tried it once. I got carried home in the arms of the principal while Mother frantically searched the town for Pete, and soon after his desk was moved to the front of the classroom. All of his objections failed to reverse the teacher's decision. At that time, Dad promised that I would soon go to kindergarten; I just needed to wait until I turned five. In Forest Lake, I asked my brothers to find out what kindergarten was like at this school. Matt came back with the news there was no kindergarten here. I would have to wait two years before I'd be old enough to start first grade. I didn't think I could make it.

That winter Mother and I spent our days alone together in the cinderblock house. It was a cold winter. She had no connections in the town, and with one exception, I don't remember her getting to know any of the neighbors. We relied on each other so much that year. She must have realized that she needed to provide a sort of kindergarten for me. She had a degree in English and music education that, of course, she did not use once she was married. Every day I wanted to play school, and eventually she asked Mrs. Nelson for primers she could use to teach me to read and do numbers. Each morning I would stand on the stairs behind the kitchen door and politely knock on the door. She would open it wide and welcome me to school. I believe we both enjoyed the lessons, our game.

After "school" and lunch, Mother would keep busy or rest, and I would nap. I remember waking up lonely. I did have Pink and Piggy, the friends who had accompanied me across the country in the form of horses. They now showed up at my side every day to play, usually in the form of small pink pigs. They were just the right size to fit next to me in a bed or chair. They lived somewhere beyond the limits of the house and went on adventures. They would bring back stories of the time they spent playing with animals; they were friends with a herd of beautiful horses and could return to their horse nature and run with them. Best of all, they could be with other children. They could go unseen into school and visit any room they liked; they told me how the children played together at recess and how they behaved in the classroom. Children. I hadn't met one yet.

I could tell when the school day was done and would go to the front door and watch at the window for a chance to spot children walking home. Mostly, though, schoolchildren rode on the bus that dropped Matt and Pete off at the corner. When a little girl walked by, I called, "Mother, a child! Can I put on my jacket and go out and play?"

"No, no, Mary. That little girl is on her way home. Her mother doesn't want her stopping at a stranger's house after school," she replied. We were strangers surrounded by strangers. The children walking by were no more than phantoms. The cold Minnesota winter, the season that fit neatly into the school year for the boys, was for me an adversary. It had arrived and settled in before me, left me with no access to the world beyond my mother and my imaginary friends. Surrounded by the winter's cold, by two imaginative brothers in a strange house, a mother with unknown worries, and a father frequently away, I grew fearful of the outside world. Inside, I remained checked, dependent on Mother, small.

Mother later would sometimes speak about how she treasured that year when she had me, her first daughter, to herself. It was a luxury not common to mothers of the time. She cared for me so well, devoted her attention to me, giving me the upbringing that she saw fit for her daughter. We grew so close. I learned how to please her, learned what was proper and right. I became her child.

The monotony of each month was broken by a trip into Minneapolis to visit the doctor. Mother and I carefully planned for each trip; we would set out our clothes the night before, completing our outfits in the morning with hats, gloves, and dark glasses.

Before each visit I would ask, "What're you going to the doctor for, Mother?"

"For a checkup, Mary."

And after each checkup I'd ask, "Are you okay, Mother?"

"Yes, I'm fine today."

I was glad she was fine, but wished I could ask a better question, one that got me a response that explained away the worry over these frequent doctor visits.

The night we met our next-door neighbors, the Forsbergs, was the night we had a roof fire. A large cinder from the coal furnace had landed on our roof and started burning. Dad was out of town at an airbase somewhere; he was on one of his field service trips for his job with Honeywell. Mother smelled smoke and hustled all of us out of the house. She knocked at the Forsbergs' house, and they took us in. Their house, quite small, surprised me by holding a beautiful grand piano. Mrs. Forsberg allowed me to touch it and press down the keys. Matt and Pete remember the siren of a fire truck, the firemen, the big hoses, and the commotion that night. What I remember about it was that we had met a neighbor family and the Forsbergs were friendly. I had met a family, and the wall of fear had been breached. Not everything here was hostile to us.

*

That old kitchen was the warm and busy heart of the house. It had an open grate in the ceiling that communicated with my bedroom above, and the smells and sounds and heat from the kitchen would waft up through it. A large ramble of a room, the kitchen was strangely broken up, as I said before, by doors and passages. The two stairway doors—one leading up to the landing, one down to the basement—were together on one wall. The basement: a decidedly unfriendly space. Like most old cellars, it smelled dank. Lit by bare bulbs hanging from the low ceiling, it was studded with large posts that were easily bumped into. A coal-burning furnace took up the center of the large open area, and there was a coal cellar back in a corner behind a large plank door. The coal cellar was dangerous, filled with a mound of black coal that men poured in through a chute from outside. We were forbidden to open the door to it. "That coal gets disturbed? It'll tumble right down on top of you. Bury you," we were warned. But the most chilling thing down in that basement was a large metal door, rarely used, hiding concrete steps that led up and outside. Matt and Pete would contrive stories of bad men who roamed the country out in the cold and who could get into the house through this unguarded opening to the outside. Even as an adult I avoided that door.

The kitchen also had a door on its front wall—a door that was covered with a heavy blanket and closed off in the winter. This led through the cinderblock wall to the summer kitchen. I had seen the summer kitchen when we first moved into the house. It was shabby, more ancient than the house itself. A stick-built addition, it was a disused space that did not resemble a kitchen at all. How strange to have a blanketed door in the kitchen to a room that didn't even feel like part of the house.

Yet the kitchen grew warmer with activity as the winter wore on. The big west window over the sink let in light on winter afternoons. Mother's energy seemed to grow. She cooked and baked more. She read the recipes aloud to me, discussing them, describing each step and its importance as she mixed and kneaded, peeled and chopped. She wiped every smudge and spill off the wide Formica counters as she worked. Even lunch was a planned event, and she would make some ceremony of it. I would set the table as she described the soup we would enjoy or the cheese on a sandwich she had put under the broiler to melt. Comforting aromas rose along with Mother's energy, and the kitchen became just the two of us, not the passages leading in and out. I forgot the warmth and the friends of California, how happiness was full of light rather than longing and a need to clutch onto Mother.

Summer did come eventually, and children living up and down the street appeared in the neighborhood. Life on our street became bright and noisy. The old stone pillars and lilac hedge were taken out that first summer, and the house lost its reputation for being haunted. The lake turned warm and watery and blue and beckoning. Forest Lake is made up of a string of three lakes, imaginatively named First, Second, and Third Lake. The south side of First Lake, where we lived, was sandy and shallow until far out at the drop-off where tall weeds grew. Even small children could splash around the sandy beach, look for shells, and learn to enjoy the fishy smell of the shore. In the spring Dad put up a dock and tied an old rowboat to it. He taught us to dig worms, put them on hooks, and fish with cane poles. He let each of us, once we proved capable of rowing, take the boat out on the lake and go exploring. We could go past the drop-off, past the bay, even as far as Second or Third Lake, though Third Lake was a long way off. No one rowed that far.

"Sure, go out as far as you want. But I can't get you home. You have to row yourselves home, you know." Dad's permission carried its own warning. We were free to push ourselves as far as we wanted; just remember that we also needed to get ourselves home.

When Mother was recovering from breast surgery, she had been cautioned that a future pregnancy could be dangerous, but by the end of spring, a doctor would confirm that she was indeed pregnant. A baby sister, Kathy, was born at the tail end of that year. A second baby, Steve, followed the next year, a year to the day from when Kathy was born.

I was worried and hoped these babies had not hurt Mother by being born. Their births had seemed fraught with danger, and Grandma and Grandpa came for a long stay to help with each. But it was Steve, not Mother, who was in grave danger at birth. He was such a tiny baby, born too early. "Small enough to fit in a shoebox," said Grandma Annie. He was stricken almost immediately with pneumonia and kept in the hospital for several weeks. It took most of that winter to nurse him to health. But eventually he thrived, and once again danger, and worry, faded.

Our family—life itself—had expanded. The five of us had a new sense of ourselves as a large family. The cold wall of isolation I had felt so keenly during the first long winter had been crumbling, little by little, starting from the first time I met the Forsbergs and touched their piano. I had responsibilities now. I was growing up, helping out in the kitchen, helping out with the babies. I finally had found friends, a whole long street full of them. It had taken a long time, but I was finally free to play, to take my place with a neighborhood gang that made up games with special rules that gave even the little kids a chance to play. We all recognized the distinctive whistle of each parent calling us home to supper in the evenings. "Jack! Carol! That's your dad. You need to go home." Every day my best friend, Karen, and I played make-believe games, swam in the lake, and rowed the boat as far as we wanted. We sometimes got caught in the rain on the far shore and rowed home wet, thrilled.

A few years later, the old kitchen got remodeled, modernized. The summer kitchen was torn down and replaced with a new room, a family room with big windows that looked onto the street. The cinderblock house became light-filled and welcoming. It accommodated crowds of friends, family celebrations, eventually wedding parties. And for a long time, I forgot that we had lived in California and that our lives had somehow changed in a way I could never quite grasp. This house was the only home I could remember.

It was only much later that I came to understand that a crisis had played out in our mother's life and in our family's. I wonder now how Mother got through those years. What fear, what desperation did she face? How did she maintain such an undisturbed demeanor? She told me once or twice of an experience she had in the hospital one night after surgery. She had awoken to see Jesus at the foot of her bed, and without words, He stood watching over her for a long while and blessed her. She said it was the most powerful religious experience of her life. Perhaps she bore the ordeal and uncertainty with outward calm because she had been given this sign of hope. I don't know. I knew her so intimately, yet I never thought to ask.

Life plays with all of us. We don't know how to divine the winds that have changed the sweep of lives, or consider the troubles carried by those around us. If we are lucky, we may live out our lives in the shelter of home and family, but that doesn't mean that we truly understand each other or know how to ask the real questions. And without those questions, who of us is willing to crack the neat veneer we've constructed of our lives? We see no more than the skeletons of each other's lives, even our deepest connections, our closest relationships, our mothers. I hold mere shards of understanding—fleeting memories veiled in the carefully composed stories told by my parents about those long ago times.

THE APPLE TREE

My sister must have noticed
I am too impatient
for anything to be long
so she tells me,
 "Write poetry, write poetry."
I say,
"I can't do it;
it's too hard."
Then I remember
my dad working in the apple tree,
telling me,
"Prune until you smile."
Now I write poetry
tight as bone
stretching out memory.

SOD FARM

Only when it rains

and grass grows

and is sold and put on lawns

of people

already fat with wealth;

only when these people

stop being thin in their payments

do we kids eat.

ORANGE

I open an orange

like a bouquet of flowers

squeeze it fully

as I love it more

now than ever before

as I remember my mother

living through the Depression

thin as wafer

eating a cheese sandwich

and an orange

with all gusto,

yet it is what I eat

when I am well

holding it

high as sacrament.

TO MOM

When we were young,

You served us kids

Oatmeal regular as Goldilocks.

You had to.

Oatmeal was what

Stuck to our stomach

For us to study.

We knew better

than to ask for more

like Oliver Twist.

If we waited for manners,

Nothing would be left.

Still, we remained

Thin as teeth until graduation.

Now that we're plum

with children,

we sit around barbecues.

MINNESOTA SUITE

—after Chu Hsi

I
Beauty
     near the lake
         goes beyond
             words.

II
Evening:
     a traveler
         sits near
            the cabin
                sipping wine.

III
The moon
      high
            above us
                  and bright.

IV
A
      single
            fisherman
                  on
                        the lake.

V
We talk
      about
            crops
                  weather
                      work.

VI
When
      the years
            come on
                  maybe
                      I'll lay
                          my pens
                            and books
                              aside.

VII
Float

on

a

fisherman's

boat.

VIII
Maybe

I'll

come

back

to

this

place.

Previously published in Minnesota Suite,
Spoon River Poetry Press, 1987

TOWARD MOORHEAD, MINNESOTA

"Held where sky touched land along the edge"
—William Stafford

Dusk. And the last miles toward home.
The dying down of the hard winds
Of the afternoon, the plumes of white
Smoke curling in the evening light,
Tell us we are at the edge of Minnesota.
Returning from the bright cities
Or the places we once called home,
We remember a story told about
Another time, when traders made
This world along other trails;
How in this valley, sleepers,
As if in a dream, were awakened
By the creaks and groans of oxcarts—
Heavy with goods—whose dry oak wheels
Rubbed ungreased axles, and echoed
Along the miles down the quiet valley.
In the rearview mirror we glimpse the dark
Behind us, then look to the road ahead,

To the final windbreak, the sure furrows
and fields reaching for the city's edge,
And then, at last, to the city, itself,
Stretching like a rosary of light, along the river,
The horizon growing wider than our dream.
Traveler, who is listening to the echoes
Of our own history, under the stars of this valley,
As we find our way through dusk
And the last miles toward home?

Previously published in Perennial Magazine. *Fall 1994*

CLOSING THE CABIN

1.

In the yawn of dusk,

we drift home in Minnesota autumn,

reciting the litany once more:

dock in; boathouse latched;

rugs rolled; plugs pulled;

windows hinged; floors swept;

pilots out; pipes drained;

faucets opened; doors locked;

hummingbird feeder taken down;

key hanging in its secret place.

2.

In the flicker of lights near the city's edge

we talk easily, gather within

all that the summer has given:

a great fish, slender and shiny,

diving for bottom; loons calling

in the still afternoon;

stars swirling above the rooftops.

Near home, vees of geese circle,

circle in the shadows above us.

3.

Later that night, we pause

on the stairs—winterward—

unlock that other season

where little puffs of winter dust

rise when we open the door.

Previously published in The University of Windsor Review. *Vol. 20, No. 2. Spring/Summer, 1987*

TURF

Between 1985 and 2003, about 4,300 miles from the American heart-land, nearly one million Danes were born, whose health records were carefully compiled for years. Clever researchers at Aarhus University in Denmark combined these records with satellite imagery of Denmark to come up with an impressive statistic: children raised near high amounts of green space have up to a 55 percent lower risk of developing mental health disorders. The researchers speculate that greener neighborhoods may reduce stress, encourage exercise, and have less noise and air pollution.

Accompanying this information in a magazine I read one afternoon is a stock photo of a girl in a pink shirt chasing a boy in a blue shirt around a tree on a grassy lawn as the sun streams down on them—children at play.

Farm. His mother was very fond of this particular photograph of her baby boy for some reason. There he lay: baby on pillow, on untamed grass, brambly bushes in the background.

Did she love how he looked straight at the photographer, or that he held his head up so well, so young? Or was it how his pudgy torso, clad in pale summer cottons, melded with the pillow? Perhaps she was taken by his limbs stretching out toward the pillow's edges. It may have been because his right toes—just out of sight, obscured by the pillow's poof—touched the rich sod on which the pillow rested.

The baby boy was my father, Keith. This grainy photograph was taken in 1919, on a farm near Junction City in eastern Kansas. My father was born in the farmhouse located just steps from this pillow. Although his family soon moved into town, my father whiled away many childhood days on this farm and another his grandfather owned. On these family farms, he greeted the animals, he roamed the fields, and he wandered along—and tumbled into—the clear flowing creek. He joined with his grandparents, parents, aunts, uncles, sister, and cousins for picnics beneath the broad shade trees. A photograph my father treasured shows thirty-nine adults and children, shoulder to shoulder, hip to hip, packed between two trees one summer afternoon when my father was about seven.

My father's love for the Schmedemann farms ran strong, but world events preempted any opportunity to build a life there. He left college to enter the Army, the European Theatre of World War II, and a three-decade career that kept him moving around the United States and the world. His career was about war, the threat of war, the building of defenses, and the protection of the country he loved.

But did he leave the farm life behind? Not completely. After years of living on Army bases, when my father could finally buy his own homes, he became an avid lawn-tender. He bought homes with good-sized lawns, each larger than the one before. He did not plant fancy beds of flowers or rows of vegetables (some fine bushes and tomato plants, yes). But he nourished his lawn, his sod, with dedication. I can still see him striding, with precision and purpose, garbed in a white T-shirt and khaki pants (both staining with sweat), back and forth across his lawn, fertilizing, mowing. He would stop at times to mop his bald head with an old golf towel, then reward himself at task's end with a frosty beer. This was his weekend heaven until, truly, his dying days at age ninety-three.

I believe the Danish study results. Of course, childhood proximity to green space bodes well for the budding adult. But aren't there more questions to be asked? Here is what I wonder: For each child, what kind of green space? How does the child experience his or her green space? How does that experience ground the budding adult?

Neighborhood. As she grew up, the parents of the ten-year-old girl in this photograph took many pictures of her in front of the white brick house with pink shutters on the well-tended lawn. This particular one is among her favorites. In this one, her curly hair is behaving, she is smiling naturally for once, and the floral dress is stylish even now. Snug beside her stands not her older sister, her usual posing partner, but rather her mother, who wears a similar floral dress. Standing by the big, black iron pot with some freshly planted azaleas makes for a nice composition. Such a lovely picture!

The ten-year-old girl is me. This slightly blurry black-and-white photograph was taken in 1966 in McLean, Virginia, where I lived for eight years of my childhood in a neighborhood named Potomac Hills. The curving streets rose and fell gently; the yards flowed one into another, equal expanses of tended grass unfettered by fences, sidewalks, mature trees, or parental wariness. A small woods with a creek beckoned at the end of our cul-de-sac; a community swimming pool nestled among the trees a few streets away.

We children roamed widely. We scooped up playmates: the Gardner quintet lived across the street; Valerie up the street, Katya and sisters Sandy and Candy down the street; Lori one street over; Janet and Betty (and her two barely tolerable brothers) on the way to the pool. We rolled through games—tag, Red Rover, pirates—until the mugginess got the better of us and we flopped exhausted on the soft grass (everyone's grass was soft), or the sun went down and the lightning bugs came out, or our parents called us home (my mother rang a cowbell).

Behind the white brick house (no pink shutters on the back) lay a miniature terrain. Our yard sloped awkwardly, so my father installed some boulders and ivy-like plants against the house to help with drainage. On shady afternoons, this swath of ground was overtaken by Barbie dolls and their compatriots. These dolls undertook daring adventures, sneaking and leaping and racing in and around the boulders.

Dolls packed up, I left Potomac Hills just as I entered my teenage years. I moved with my family; I grew into adulthood.

Or rather: I thought I left Potomac Hills. But in maturity, I have realized that Potomac Hills lingers in me. As an Army officer's child who lived in six places by the time I graduated from high school, I am stumped by the question, "Where are you from?" I often answer, "I lived different places growing up." My nuanced answer would be: "I am from Potomac Hills." It was Potomac Hills that gave me my place-based identity, that made me a searching girl. In Potomac Hills, I learned to wander far and wide, to seek out other people, to engage with them, to create our activities, to concoct our stories—to invent myself. From this neighborhood, I went on to study three foreign languages, study on both coasts, earn two graduate degrees, become a lawyer and law professor, travel the world, and raise two oh so independent daughters.

Yard. Her mother keeps this photograph on her bedroom dresser. Evening's shadow is but inches from overtaking her corn-silk curls; the day's last light shines on her slight smile and steadfast chocolate eyes, a serious face for a four-year-old. She holds her impish baby sister, dressed in a sweet pink romper, tight to her chest. They sit at the top of their banana-yellow slide, firmly bolted into their elaborate wood "play structure." Its sturdy beams frame this scene against the cobalt sky. It is nearly time to come in for their bath.

The four-year-old girl is Mary, my daughter. This crystal-clear photograph was taken in 1988 in Woodbury, Minnesota, a suburb of St. Paul. Mary spent countless hours over nine years of her childhood on that play structure situated in a bed of sand in our spacious backyard, framed by a rectangle of green chain-link fence. Though lightweight and long limbed, Mary grew strong as she climbed the ladders, swung across the monkey bars, pumped on the swings, and dug in the sand for hours at a time. She and her sister were often joined by two sisters from next door and two girls from across the street. In pairs and trios and quartets, they would slip in and out of improv skits as though the bed of sand were a stage.

Once Mary, her sister, and three of their playmates ran away. Beforehand, they packed lunches and cameras in two backpacks, then alerted me and the mother next door to their upcoming departure. They went as far as the community park—just on the other side of our fence. There they ate their lunches, posed for pictures, and chatted conspiratorially. We mothers watched from inside our houses, bemused.

Mary left that yard for good before eighth grade. Our next family home, in the city of Minneapolis, featured a large deck instead of a backyard. Her strong limbs formed on that sturdy play structure served her well as she excelled in high school cross-country running, track, and cross-country skiing. And our house filled with the sounds of her new gal-pals. In due course, Mary moved a few states east to attend college in a first-ring suburb of Chicago, a community not so different from Minneapolis. I saw her there so easily.

Then she moved into Chicago. Mary would start this paragraph with "and"; I would choose "but." Such a large city, I thought: so complex, so crowded, so compressed, so concrete. I worried. Would her soul be stifled?

No. Mary has thrived there for over a decade. I have gradually come to see that Mary's childhood in our Woodbury yard has given Mary a place-based identity of her own. Mary is a settling girl, a woman who has the self-security to bloom in this cityscape. Wherever she is, she finds what she needs within herself, within the resources near at hand and the people she draws close to her, within what she soon makes familiar. In Chicago, she has spun a life based on her inner strength and her web of connections: a close circle of friends, a newly founded church, a community in her apartment building, the local farmers markets and community nonprofits with which she works. And yes, she and her family know every green space, every park within walking and biking distance of their apartment.

Farm Revisited. What of my father? How did his childhood forays to the family farms ground him? In his later years, my father dictated his life story. He spoke of the farms as places that sustained his family—a literally true point when his elders ate the products grown on their land. As I think back on my father's life, I see that the time he spent on the family farms planted in him a view of the world as benevolent: a place where God bestows beauty, life unfolds organically and seasonally, and people gather in harmony. This benevolent world view provided him spiritual sustenance for what was to come: the Depression, service as a soldier in World War II (including discovery of the Jewish internees in Buchenwald), command duty in Korea, the demoralization of the Vietnam War, the vexing illnesses of his precious daughters, and twice becoming a widower. Through all of this, he steadfastly believed that good is present, always and everywhere.

In late midlife, my father returned to live in Kansas. Even though ownership of the family farms had long since passed from Schmedemann hands, he visited the farm where an icehouse had once stood next to the farmhouse. The walls of that icehouse were formed of hand-hewn limestone blocks from the area. My father brought two of those limestone blocks back to anchor his final front yard. Onto one of them he affixed his house number: 8632.

Upon his death, I took possession of that limestone block. It could weigh close to a hundred pounds, I calculated when I decided to move it north. With great effort, my husband managed to position it in a perfect spot near our lake-side cabin. The other day, I noticed that the numbers are peeling off. The "cabin grass" in our yard, I must admit, is quite unruly. Some errant greenery has migrated onto the limestone and is undermining the adhesive. I have yet to decide whether to stick the numbers back on—or to let nature, whimsical, winsome nature, take her course.

DRIVING NORTH

You are drawn to the lake

as if it waited for you to return,

as if the continent leaned north

itself and you had no choice

but to follow the ruts and washboard road.

Now, in late August, somewhere

along the Canadian border trees grow

like hooks, the last dandelions molt,

wild asparagus waves its ferny head

to claim no one has travelled this far,

but you know what time and weather

will do with every leaf. The endless

rubbing of water on broken glass.

Every season has its cruelties,

yet driving north makes you

forget the questions that weigh

upon you in your mind. How instantly

suffering stops—you don't have time

for guilt, nor care to remember the way back

home, because there is always something

larger than you, liquid, unlived, the lake

widespread, drifting away from shore.

LAKE OF THE WOODS

I've gazed at the same sky and same ceiling
of stars from the same dock wondering
what I want from life, and perhaps, if I had not
left so soon, so many years ago, but stayed here,
by now I would have trained my eyes to recognize
what I was seeking—the barbs on the vane
of a pinion feather, muskrats resting in elegant reeds,
the diaspora of pine cones under the trees.

1997: BAUDETTE, MN

~ *after MRB Chelko*

Year of the Great Flood. Year of snow
and ice always falling. Year the lake
swallowed boats, docks, and shorelines.
Year of my first date at Rosalie's—the only
restaurant in town. Year the jar of honey
fell from my hands to the ground—
the sticky mess spreading slowly at my feet.
The glass I couldn't save from breaking.

Year the neighbor shot our dog—
the dog's body a hurricane of pain,
laboring to breathe, unable to stand.
Afternoon my father, alone, carried it
out to the woods in a brown blanket.
We ate fish for dinner, my father silent,
as the family pretended not to notice
the dog's absence.

Year I waited for the town to stop gossiping
how my friend, Nick, must have been drunk

when his car went off the road and into the ditch.

Ten years after, he waited for the probation
officer to stop calling to "check in." Fifteen years
after Nick's still not aware, always clinging
to a bottle, always lungs clouded with nicotine.
The car now parked sits motionless
like an animal crouched in long grass.

Year of cold air in the empty house:
my father backing out of the driveway
at 5:00 a.m., escaping to work;
my brother moved to the Twin Cities.

Year my mother planted a red maple
near the house. Twenty years after
the branches brush against the window.
The tree grows in an upright position,
bending with the wind and shifting earth,
reminding me how strong I have to be
to keep from falling.

Fiction
by Kristin Laurel

TERMINAL BURROWING

But he was not buried in Minneapolis
At least.
And no more may I be
Please God. ~ *James Wright*

Handsome Sven's on the TV, jabbering about the weather. He says it's been the coldest winter in decades, but I don't need a meteorologist to tell me that. All I have to do is take a look outside my window: You've never seen an old dog look more pitiful trying to pee fast and not sink into a six-foot snowdrift.

I've spent over half of my life in this state, but even James Wright couldn't hack it. I wish he would have gotten out of Minneapolis more; he might have liked it better in Waconia. Out here, there's hot coffee and donuts at every gas station from here to Ortonville. Out here, there's a community of ice houses on every frozen lake. Even though there's more drinking than writing poetry in there, you have to admire them for being creative. I should hate it here, but I don't.

It's true. I haven't seen a neighbor in months, but at the grocery store today a tall gray-bearded man with a staff in his hand held the door open. He looked so wise and reminded me of Gandalf (except for the purple Vikings sweatshirt). His lips were dry and cracked, and even though it must have hurt, he smiled. Meanwhile, over in the produce section, I overheard a young woman say, "It sure is cold, but at least the sun is shining." And then I heard another woman with the voice of my grandma say, "Today's the kind of day to stay home and make soup."

I let the dog back in, shut the TV off, and warm up my soup. I wrap myself up in my blanket and sink into the couch. I pick up a magazine and find an article about hypothermia. It says that in the final stages of hypothermia, humans have been known to dig themselves into a hole and die. It's called "terminal burrowing," and it has something to do with the brainstem shutting down. Well now, that's one heck of a metaphor. That explains everything.

"Terminal Burrowing" was originally published in The Talking Stick, *Vol. 24*

THE FARM

~For Howard and Lenore Graff

i.

My ten-year-old son asks on the drive
to the nursing home:
"Why can't Grandpa remember?"
They sit next to each other on the bed,
and count the twenty ones
in my grandfather's wallet
over and over again.
Then great-grandfather hands
the wallet to great-grandson and says:
"If I give ya all I got, will ya take me back to the farm?"

ii.

I ran away—
at least that's what it felt like.
Not like when my fed-up father
stuck me on a Greyhound,
at thirteen, for a five-day trip
from California to Minnesota.
I got offered a Quaalude in Barstow,
met a pimp and a nice old couple
in a bus depot in Omaha.
I only had enough money to choose
between food or cigarettes,
so I smoked,
gave a beggar a candy bar,
threw away some change in a slot machine near Vegas
just to feel like I was losing.

iii.

I jumped off that bus
dressed in black with spiked-up hair
and landed in my grandmother's arms.
While the small-town people stared,
she took me to the Dairy Queen, the library,
and then home—
to a world without rancor,
a three-bedroom farmhouse
surrounded by pine and a fresh coat of white paint.

iv.

My first memory is on the farm;

crawling around as a toddler on the kitchen floor,

following the circular designs on the linoleum like a map;

Mom and Grandma sitting at the breakfast nook

their voices lingering, the aroma of coffee and toast.

Outside, hundreds of acres of soybean, wheat, and corn,

a swing set where a kid could sing and scream,

an old pink shack to play house, a grove to run in and get clothes dirty,

where deer and squirrels hid, but would poke out their heads

just to get a glimpse of my grandma's garden, her purple irises.

v.

A voice reading a eulogy.

The suffocation of held-back tears.

She would have been surprised

at the packed church, all these people, making such a fuss.

They say she was a woman of faith,

a dedicated wife of a Norwegian farmer,

who cooked and cleaned and ironed

and taught ceramics in her basement.

They don't know my grandmother like I did.

They haven't played dot-to-dot with the freckles on her hands,

slept with her on that pool table she called a firm mattress,

stayed up late just to feel the excitement of a summer storm.

They don't know that she kept a journal,

painted canvas with oil, studied Native American history,

and taught me, "Don't believe everything you read in
school."

She played the organ, the harmonica, she sang the blues.

They never saw her throw a crouton across the table at the
Olive Garden

or sit on the curb in San Antonio at Sea World,

unbutton her blouse and fan herself in the hot Texas heat
and say,

"I'm a member of AARP, I get to do anything I want."

They don't know there were days when she wanted off that
farm—because it did not define her,

because she was so much more.

vi.

Easter Sunday.

He is ninety today.

Sitting hunched over in his chair

in this Alzheimer's unit

surrounded by a family of strangers—

It is time to pray.

My grandfather taught me the Lord's Prayer,

and to love good topsoil; he stood among his rows of soybeans,

his back to the sun, scooping chunks of black dirt into his
palm,

rubbing it until it crumbled, and fell between the spaces of
his fingers.

He set me loose with a machete at eight years old,

to chop down weeds,

and I almost cut off my finger.

My left index fingernail still grows slanted

like the roof of the barn

where I would crawl into the loft,

where it was dark and dank and felt forbidden,

smelling of gasoline, grease, manure, and hay.

He taught me to listen

to the sound of faraway thunder,

to the melody of a finely tuned tractor,

to the radio, especially the weather.

He taught me to drive a stick shift,

then he pulled me out of the ditch.

He taught me how to sweat

and work and love the dirt of this earth.

He told me I was the best little worker he ever had—

He told my cousins the same thing.

He taught me how to find my way back home

if I get lost in rows of corn.

vii.

I've never lived in one place for more than five years.

Now I live in the town where I was born.

I hope to stay, until these kids are grown.

I want to teach them to bake like my grandmother, tell them,
"the secret's in the measuring and the mixing."
I want them to know contentment, like my grandfather had,
with himself, and God, and his love for the land.
I want to show them some consistency in an inconsistent
world.
I am divorced. I hate to cook
Yet, when the kids get off the school bus and come home
at least they get to be themselves every day.
Some would say I'm undisciplined.
I've tried on a few roles, dabbled with some things…
Yet, I am slowly learning
how to live, like a kid on the farm.

Previously published in Giving Them All Away*, Evening Street
Press (2012)*

FIRELIGHT

Jimmy hadn't planned to break the windows; he hadn't thought about it at all. He'd just been walking around the neighborhood, as he always did on the Saturdays his mother's boyfriend came to town. He'd left the apartment so quickly that he'd forgotten his mittens, and he walked with his hands balled in his jacket pockets. He thought about going back to get his mittens, but once when he'd gone home before he was supposed to, his mother and her boyfriend were in her bedroom with the door closed, making noises. He knew what those noises meant because one day at recess a third-grader named Evan was talking about what grown-ups do in bedrooms. "It's the same as dogs," he'd said. Jimmy couldn't imagine his mother doing such a thing with anybody, especially that vacuum salesman from St. Paul with his thick glasses and hairy ears. And maybe she didn't do it after all. Maybe they were in her bedroom because she was too tired to sit up in the living room and talk. She was always tired, even though she didn't work at the café anymore, and she spent most days in bed anyway. But what were the noises then?

He tried to think of something else. He thought about the Teenage Mutant Ninja Turtles and the frog his friend Greg brought to school in a jar once and let loose in the lunchroom. Michael Jackson kept a brain in a jar in his bedroom, and Greg said that proved he was crazy. But Jimmy thought he probably just wished he could put that person's brain in his head, and that didn't seem crazy to him. But maybe that was because he was crazy too. If he had Greg's brain, he'd know if he was or not. He imagined lying in bed with Greg's brain in his head and his own brain in a jar on the dresser and wondered what he'd think. But he couldn't guess. If his brain was normal, shouldn't he be able to guess what someone else would think?

His mother's brain definitely wasn't normal. Ever since his father left them, she'd had to take pills for her mind. Jimmy used to blame the way she was on his father, but maybe she wasn't much different before he left. His father used to call her a crazy bitch, so maybe that was why he left, because she was crazy even then. Jimmy didn't know. He couldn't remember much about that time because he was so little. He barely even remembered his father. He just remembered that he was tall and had a mustache and smoked brown cigarettes. And he remembered how his big hands would hurt him when he picked him up under his arms, and how he liked him to pick him up anyway. Jimmy wondered where his father was now and what he was doing. His mother said he lived in Nebraska with his new family, and Jimmy wondered if Nebraska was a town or a state and how far away it was. And did his father ever pick up his new son the way he used to pick him up?

He was tired of walking around, so he decided to go over to the school playground. Kids were always there on weekends, playing on the swings and monkey bars or tossing a football back and forth. But when he got to the playground, no one was there. Even the houses across the street seemed deserted. Everywhere he looked, there was nothing. Not even a stray dog. And suddenly he felt all alone. A long shiver snaked up his spine, and he wanted to go home and sit on the edge of his mother's bed and talk to her. But it wasn't six o'clock yet. Her boyfriend would still be there.

He started walking slowly toward home anyway, kicking rocks as he crossed the gravel playground. But when he rounded the south wing of the school, he stopped. The sun was setting in the long row of windows, making them glow with a beautiful, cold fire. He'd seen those windows many times before, but only today did he realize how easy it would be to break one. All you had to do was pick up a rock and throw it. Anybody could do it, but nobody ever did. Maybe you had to be crazy to do it. He picked up a rock to see if he would throw it. What would Greg think if he saw him now? Would he try to talk him out of it? And what about his mother and his father? What would they say? Jimmy imagined his father walking down the sidewalk and seeing him with the rock in his hand. "Hey, Jimmy," he'd say. "Is that you?"

Then one of the windows exploded, and Jimmy jumped back, startled, and looked at his empty hand. He couldn't remember throwing the rock, but he had. And now that he'd done it, he felt so good, so suddenly happy, that he kept on picking up rocks and throwing them, breaking window after window, until he heard a car coming down the street and had to run away.

*

By Monday morning, when Jimmy went back to school, the janitors had swept up the glass and taped cardboard over the eighteen broken windows. After the bell rang, all the kids in his class were still standing by the windows, talking excitedly about who could have done it, and they didn't take their seats until Mrs. Anthony threatened to keep them inside during recess. And even before the class could recite the Pledge of Allegiance, the principal's voice came over the loudspeaker and said the guilty party would eventually be caught, so he might as well turn himself in now. The guilty party—that was Jimmy. He tried not to look guilty, but the more he tried, the more he felt everyone knew he had done it. Ever since he'd broken the windows, he'd felt like a stranger in his own life, someone just pretending to be who he was, and he was sure everyone would see the change in his face if they looked. He stared at his desk intently, as if merely to look up would be a confession.

Later that morning, as the class was on its way out for recess, Mrs. Anthony stopped him at the door and asked if she could talk to him for a minute. He was sure then that she had found out, but when the others were gone, she only asked if he was feeling all right. He nodded. Her forehead furrowed then, and he looked away. "Jimmy," she said. "You can tell me. Have things been bad at home again?" Her husky voice was soft, like his mother's when she was trying to make up for something she'd said. Somehow it made him angry. "Yes," he lied, and the word seemed to take his breath away. "My mother was mean to me." And then he ran outside and sat under a maple tree near the swings, trying to get his breath back. Greg came over then and challenged him to a game of tetherball, but Jimmy said he didn't want to play. "Why not?" Greg said. "You chicken?" And even though Greg started to flap his arms and cluck like a chicken, Jimmy did not get up and chase him.

School ended that day without anyone accusing him of breaking the windows, but he was still certain he'd be caught. Maybe somebody already knew, but they hadn't said anything because they were testing him, trying to see if he would confess on his own. He didn't know what to think. It was like he had to learn a whole new way of thinking now that he'd broken the windows. As he walked home, he tried out different things to say when he was accused. He could say it was all an accident— he'd been trying to hit some blackbirds that were flying past or something—or maybe there was a robber, somebody breaking into the school, and he'd chased him away by throwing rocks at him and some of them hit the windows. But nothing he thought of sounded good enough, and after a while he gave up and tried to think of something else.

Though the afternoon was bright and sunny, the temperature had dropped below freezing. He hunched his shoulders against the cold and started down the street to the rundown clapboard house where he and his mother rented an apartment on the second floor. He was hoping his mother wasn't too tired to make hot chocolate for him. But then he saw the social worker's yellow Subaru parked in front of the house again and knew he wouldn't get any hot chocolate—or even any supper. After Mrs. McClure's visits, his mother was always so exhausted she'd have to go to bed for the rest of the day, and he'd have to make his own supper and hers too. And that meant he'd have to eat hot dogs or toast again because they were the only things he could cook. And he'd have to watch TV by himself all night too, and every now and then he'd probably hear her crying in her room. He knew better than to go in and try to comfort her, though; that only made her cry harder or, sometimes, yell at him.

He didn't want to go inside while Mrs. McClure was there, but it was so cold he went in the dark, musty entryway of the old house and climbed the steps up to the second-floor landing. Outside their apartment he hesitated a moment, then opened the door quietly. He hoped he could sneak through the kitchen and down the hall to his room without Mrs. McClure seeing him. Carefully he set his book bag on the rug and hung his jacket on the coatrack. Then he heard his mother's voice coming from the living room.

"So I had a glass with lunch. I don't know what's the big hairy deal. Who appointed you my savior anyway?"

"Now, Marjorie, I don't think of myself as—"

"Look, why don't you just get the hell out of here. I'm sick to death of your stupid face. Just get out and leave me alone."

During the silence that followed, Jimmy's jacket suddenly slipped off the coatrack and landed with a muffled thud on the floor. "Jimmy?" his mother said. "Is that you?"

Jimmy sighed. "Yes," he said and stepped to the doorway of the living room.

Mrs. McClure turned in her chair. "Why, hello, Jimmy! Aren't you getting to be a big boy?" She said things like that every time she saw him, as if she hadn't seen him just the week before. He hated that, and hated even more the times she tried to act like she was his mother. Last month, when it was time for parent-teacher conferences, she'd gone to his school and talked to Mrs. Anthony about the Unsatisfactory he got in Conduct. She had no right to do that; that was his mother's job, not hers.

"Aren't you going to say hello, Jimmy?" Mrs. McClure said.

"Hi," Jimmy answered. But that didn't satisfy her; she kept looking at him, as if she were waiting for him to say something else, and he thought again how her long nose and chin made her look like a witch.

"Come on in and sit down," she said then, as if it were her apartment, but Jimmy stayed in the doorway. Finally, she turned back to his mother, who was lying on the couch in her flannel nightgown and blue terrycloth bathrobe, an arm crooked over her eyes to block out the light slanting through the tall windows. Mrs. McClure always opened the drapes when she came. "No wonder you're down in the dumps," she'd say. "You keep this place too dark." Now she said, "I suppose I should be going. But don't forget what I said about a new hairdo. I think you'd be surprised how much better you'd feel about yourself." She nodded her bangs at his mother's greasy brown hair to emphasize her point. "And the Rosary Society at St. Jacob's is sponsoring a clothing drive. Perhaps you'd like me to bring around a few things in your size?" Jimmy looked at Mrs. McClure and tried to imagine his mother wearing her pink dress and nylons, her hoop earrings and silver and turquoise bracelets. But he couldn't, and he started to giggle. He didn't think it was funny, but he started to giggle anyway.

"Shush," his mother said without removing her arm from her eyes. Some days that was the only thing she said to him. She got headaches easily, so he had to be quiet around her. Sometimes he even watched TV with the sound off, guessing at what people were saying. It was kind of fun, watching the mouths move and no sounds come out, and sometimes in school he'd pretend he was deaf and dumb until Mrs. Anthony threatened to send him to the principal's office. Just thinking about how red Mrs. Anthony's face got when she was mad made him giggle more. He wished he could have seen her face when he first saw all the broken windows. He imagined it getting so red that steam blew out her ears, just like in the cartoons, and he started laughing. His mother gritted her teeth. "I said stop it." But he couldn't stop.

Mrs. McClure turned to look at him, her head tilted a little, like a bird listening for worms underground, and he began laughing hard. But then—he didn't know how it happened—he was crying. His mother didn't get up, but she pointed at him. "Now look what you've done," she said to Mrs. McClure.

"Look what I've done?" Mrs. McClure said. "Can't you see why he's crying? He's just come home from school, and you haven't even said hello to him. All you've done is snap at him."

"Why don't you just shut the fuck up."

"I have a job to do, Marjorie, and I intend to do it. But if you're not interested in helping yourself, how can I possibly help you?"

His mother sat up slowly and leaned toward Mrs. McClure. "You can help me by getting the hell out of my apartment."

"Marjorie, you know that—"

"I said get out."

Mrs. McClure sighed and shook her head, then she turned to Jimmy. "Don't cry, honey," she said. "Everything's going to work out in the end." She held out her arms. "Come here, sweetie."

For a second, he saw himself sitting in her lap, her arms around him, and he almost started toward her. That fact surprised him so much he stopped crying.

Mrs. McClure dropped her arms and sat there a moment, looking at him, then she slowly stood up. "Maybe I've done all I can do here," she said to his mother. "Maybe it's time to take your case to another level."

His mother glared at her. "Just what is that supposed to mean?" she asked. But Mrs. McClure only shook her head, then gathered up her manila folder and purse and started toward the door.

"You and your damned threats," his mother said to her back. "You can just go to hell."

Mrs. McClure didn't answer. She merely stopped for a second to tousle Jimmy's curly black hair and say, "Don't worry, we'll take care of you." Then she went out the door and down the steps.

"'A new hairdo,'" his mother said then. "She can just go fuck herself." Jimmy looked at her. Normally her round face was pale and her eyes looked wet, as if she had just finished crying or was about to start, but now her skin was splotchy and her eyes looked fierce. "What are you staring at?" she said.

Jimmy wanted to ask what Mrs. McClure meant by "another level," but he didn't dare. "Do you want me to make you supper tonight?" Jimmy asked. "I can make hot dogs if we got some."

"Just shut the damned drapes," she said. "Shut all the goddamned drapes and leave me alone. I'm tired and I want to sleep." She lay back on the sagging couch and hugged herself. "And get me a blanket. It's cold in here."

"Okay," Jimmy said and went around the room closing the drapes. Then he got a spare blanket from the linen closet and started to cover his mother with it. Her eyes were closed and he thought she was already asleep, but she opened them and said, "You're a good boy, Jimmy. I'm not mad at you. You know that, don't you?" When he nodded, she gave him the smile he loved so, the one that made her eyes crinkle up. "It's you and me, kid," she said. "You and me against the world." And then she closed her eyes again and turned toward the back of the couch.

*

For the next two weeks, no one mentioned the windows, and Jimmy began to believe he wouldn't be caught after all. Then one day he came home from school and heard his mother talking on the phone in the kitchen. "Think about Jimmy," she was saying, her voice wavering. "He doesn't deserve this." Then she was silent a long time before she said, "I'll be there. Just give me a chance to explain." When she hung up, he went into the kitchen. His legs felt funny, as if his knees had turned to water. He was sure she'd been talking to the principal, or maybe a policeman.

"Oh, you're home," she said, and wiped her nose with a Kleenex.

He was about to tell her it wasn't true, someone else broke the windows, when she suddenly said, "Look at this mess!" She gestured at the dirty dishes piled on the table and counters. "We've got to clean up everything right away." Then she began to fill the sink with water, but before it was even half-full, she abruptly turned off the faucet. "We'd better do the bedrooms first," she said and hurried to her room, where she started picking up clothes and newspapers and empty wine jugs from the floor. "Just look at all of this!" she said. She carried the load out into the living room and dumped it on the sofa. Then she straightened the sofa pillows and wiped dust off the coffee table with her palm. "Don't just stand there," she said. "Help me clean up this mess!"

"What should I do?"

"You can do the dishes while I do the laundry." She led him back into the kitchen. "First," she said. But then she closed her eyes and shook her head slowly back and forth. "Oh, God, why did they have to come today? Just a half-gallon of milk and a jar of jelly in the fridge. And me still in bed . . ." Then she looked at Jimmy. Her eyes were red and swollen, and he could smell the wine on her breath. "Damn it," she said. "Who the hell do they think they are?"

Jimmy realized then that the principal and the policeman must have come to the apartment looking for him. That frightened him, but he was relieved his mother seemed madder at them than at him. She must not believe that he broke the windows. Maybe she thought he was too normal to do it, and maybe that meant he really was normal. She was his mother and she would know, wouldn't she? "What's wrong?" he finally dared to say.

"Nothing," she answered. "Nothing for you to worry about." Then she said, "To hell with the dishes. We'll do them tomorrow." And she went to bed and stayed there the rest of the night. Every now and then Jimmy heard her crying, and then she'd begin cursing. Finally she fell asleep, and Jimmy lay in his bed across the hall, listening to her peaceful breathing and wishing he could dream whatever she was dreaming so he'd know what could make her happy.

The next morning his mother surprised him by coming in to the kitchen in a lacy lavender dress with puffy sleeves. Her hair was combed, and she had put on lipstick and rouge. She frowned and said, "Do I look all right?"

"You look pretty," Jimmy said and took a bite of his toast.

"But do I look like a good mommy?" she asked. "Do I look like I clean my house and go to church and love you more than anything in the world?"

He started to smile, thinking she was teasing him, but the frightened look on her face made him stop. He looked down at his plate.

"I think so," he said.

*

All that week and most of the next, his mother dressed up each morning and left the apartment. She was looking for a new job, she told him, but every afternoon when he came home from school and asked her if she'd found one, she said no. "But I'll keep trying," she said one day, then knelt down and hugged him tightly. "I won't give up. No matter how hard I have to fight, I won't give up."

But eventually she stopped dressing in the morning and started staying in bed all day, drinking wine, just as she had before. When Jimmy asked her why she wasn't looking for jobs anymore, she said, "What are you talking about?" Then she said, "Oh, that. Forget about that. There aren't any jobs for bad mommies, not a single one."

Then one morning Mrs. McClure came to the apartment for the first time in weeks. It took Jimmy a few minutes to realize she had come to take him away. "You're going to live somewhere else for just a little while," his mother said, her voice quivering. "It's all for your own good." Then she took his small face in her hands and kissed him goodbye. "Remember I love you," she said, and her mouth twisted as if the words made it hurt. "Now go." Then Mrs. McClure took his hand and led him outside to her car.

It was several months before Jimmy learned he had not been taken away from his mother because of the windows. That morning, though, he believed they had finally proved he'd done it, and because he was too young to go to jail, they were punishing him by sending him to some stranger's house where they would watch him to make sure he didn't break any more windows. As he rode away from his home, he thought of telling Mrs. McClure he was innocent, but he was sure a teacher or janitor had seen him. And he knew that none of the excuses he had made up would work. So he didn't say anything; he just sat there, looking straight ahead while Mrs. McClure went on and on about Mr. and Mrs. Kahlstrom and how they had fixed up their spare room just for him. "They've painted the walls sea blue, and they've put a huge toy box at the foot of the bed and filled it with Transformers and Lincoln Logs and everything else you can think of," she said. "How does that sound?" When he didn't answer, she said, "You don't have anything to worry about, Jimmy. Everything's going to be just fine. You know that, don't you?" Jimmy nodded so she'd leave him alone. "That's good," she said. "I'm glad you're being such a big, brave boy."

But at the Kahlstroms' house, he wasn't brave for long. Standing in the entryway, Mrs. McClure cheerfully introduced him to the strangers who would be his temporary parents. Mrs. Kahlstrom was a small, bird-boned woman, and even though the house was warm and she was wearing a bulky turtleneck sweater, she kept hugging herself as if she were cold. She said, "Hello, Jimmy," and smiled so big he could see her gums. Mr.

Kahlstrom shook his hand when he said hello. He was tall and thin and had an Adam's apple like Ichabod Crane in the story Mrs. Anthony had read to Jimmy's class. Jimmy was so scared he wanted to turn and run out the door, but his legs were trembling too much. He didn't know what to do, and he surprised himself as much as the others when he suddenly lay down on the rug and curled up like a dog going to sleep. The three adults hovered over him, startled looks on their faces. From the floor they looked so different; it was almost as if they weren't people at all but some strange creatures from another world. Mrs. McClure took his elbow and asked him to please stand up like a good boy, but he jerked his arm away. They all tried to talk him into getting up, but he stayed on the floor, even when Mr. and Mrs. Kahlstrom tried to tempt him into the house by showing him some of the toys they'd bought. Finally Mrs. McClure said it might be best just to let him lay there until he was ready to get up. "I don't know what to say," she told the Kahlstroms. "I've never seen a reaction like this." Mrs. Kahlstrom offered him a sofa pillow then, but he shook his head, so she just set it on the linoleum beside him. Then Mrs. McClure shook their hands and said goodbye, and Mr. and Mrs. Kahlstrom went into the living room to wait for Jimmy to get up and join them.

For a time after Mrs. McClure left, Jimmy could hear them whispering. Then he heard a sudden sharp sob, and Mr. Kahlstrom saying, "There, there, dear. Just give him time." Then they went into another room, farther away, and he couldn't hear them anymore. After a while, a phone rang somewhere, and Jimmy heard Mr. Kahlstrom answer it, then say, "No, not yet" and "We'll let you know as soon as anything happens" and "Thanks for calling." A long time later, Mr. Kahlstrom came, squatted down on his haunches, and set a plate beside the rug. "It's lunchtime, Jimmy," he said. "Mrs. McClure told us you liked sloppy joes and potato chips. I hope that's right." When Jimmy didn't say anything, he let out a long sigh, then stood up and went away. Jimmy was hungry, but he wasn't going to eat anything until they took him back home. He'd starve himself, and if that didn't work, he'd just break all the windows in the house. And if Mrs. McClure took him somewhere else, he'd break all the windows there too; he'd break all the windows everywhere until she'd finally have to take him back to his mother again.

A half-hour later, when Mr. Kahlstrom returned, Jimmy still hadn't eaten anything, but he was sitting up now and crying. "I'm sorry," he said. "I won't break any of your windows, I promise. Just let me go home, please. Please let me go home."

Mr. Kahlstrom knelt down beside Jimmy. "Sorry? You don't have anything to be sorry about. And you don't have to worry about breaking any of our windows or anything else either. Just feel free to play and do everything you do in your own house. And if something does break, don't worry about it—we can get it fixed. All right?"

Jimmy looked at him. Maybe he didn't know about the windows, maybe Mrs. McClure didn't tell either of them. "All right," he said.

"Say," Mr. Kahlstrom said, "I bet your sloppy joe is cold. What do you say we head into the kitchen and make you another one?"

*

For the next two months, whenever Mrs. McClure asked, Jimmy told her that he liked living with the Kahlstroms. And mostly he did. Mr. Kahlstrom taught music at the high school, and he played songs for Jimmy on the big upright piano in the living room. Jimmy's favorite was one called "Down at Papa Joe's." Mr. Kahlstrom showed Jimmy how to play the melody—he took his small hand with his big one and helped him poke out the notes with one finger—and Jimmy liked that. But he didn't like it when Mrs. Kahlstrom sat down on the corner of the piano bench beside them. She had scared him his third night there, when she tucked him into bed, by telling him that she and Roger—that was what she called Mr. Kahlstrom—had once had a little boy very much like him but that he had caught some disease called leukemia and died. It had been eleven years since he died and they still missed him, and that was why they had decided to become foster parents. She reached out her bony hand when she said that and brushed the hair away from his forehead. "He had curly hair too," she said, "only his was blond."

The Kahlstroms were nice to him. Mr. Kahlstrom took him up to the high school on weekends and let him play with all the different drums in the band room, and he bought him a Nerf football so they could play goal line stand in the living room. Mrs. Kahlstrom worried about the furniture and lamps, but she let them play anyway, and when Jimmy tackled Mr. Kahlstrom, she'd clap and say, "Way to go, Jimmy!" Mrs. Kahlstrom made him bacon and eggs for breakfast nearly every day and helped him with his homework and took him to the matinee on Saturdays, but she was so nervous all the time that she made him nervous too. And she was always talking about love. She had loved him even before she met him, she said. And at night, after she read him a story, she'd kiss him on his nose just like he was a little kid still and say she loved, loved, loved him so much she could eat him up. Then she'd sit there a moment, as if she were waiting for him to say "I love you" back, before she'd finally get up and turn out the lights. And the stories she read bothered him too. They were stupid stories, little kid stories. Once she read one about a dog that was on the ark with Noah. The dog seemed to think the flood came along just so he could have a good time, sailing around and playing games with the other animals. He never even thought about all the dogs that got drowned. His own parents had probably drowned in the flood, and his brothers and sisters too. But he didn't seem to care. And when the flood was over and Noah picked him for his pet, he jumped up and down like he was the luckiest dog in history.

*

Each Friday, Mrs. McClure came to visit for a few minutes. She never mentioned the windows, but Jimmy knew she hadn't forgotten about them because she always told him he couldn't go home just yet. He wished she'd tell him how long he was going to be punished, but all she'd ever say was, "It won't be much longer now, sweetheart." At first he thought he'd have to stay at the Kahlstroms' for eighteen days—one for each window—but when the eighteenth day came and went without her coming to take him home, he began to worry it'd be eighteen weeks. But then, a few days before Christmas, she called and told him to pack his things because she was coming to take him home. At the door, Mr. Kahlstrom shook his hand and hugged him. "Be good, Jimmy," he said, patting his back. Mrs.

Kahlstrom wasn't there; she was upstairs in her room, and although he couldn't hear her, Jimmy knew she was crying. "Tell Mrs. Kahlstrom . . ." he said, but he didn't know what he wanted him to tell her, so he stopped. Then Mrs. McClure took his hand and led him down the sidewalk to her car. He wanted to turn around and see if Mrs. Kahlstrom was watching from her window upstairs, but he didn't.

On the way home, Mrs. McClure mentioned that his mother had been at a hospital in St. Paul. "What was she doing there?" he asked.

"Getting better," Mrs. McClure answered. "Wait till you see her. She's a new person now."

And she was, too, at least for a while. His first day back, she told him he was the best Christmas present she had ever gotten, and she baked a turkey and made mashed potatoes and gravy. And afterward, she gave him a present—"Just one for now," she said. "You'll have to wait till Christmas Eve for the rest." It was a Nerf football, just like the one Mr. Kahlstrom had bought for him. He looked at her. Her chin was trembling. "Mrs. McClure told me you liked playing football," she said. "I thought maybe we could play a little sometime."

They only played a couple of times, though, before she started getting tired again. The first Saturday after Christmas she went to bed right after breakfast. Jimmy watched cartoons in the living room all morning, then made himself a peanut-butter-and-jelly sandwich for lunch. After he finished it, he went into her room to ask her if she wanted something to eat too. She was standing in front of her bureau mirror. She was still in her nightgown, but she was wearing a strange white hat with a pink ribbon around its brim. Jimmy wasn't sure, but he thought he'd seen that hat before. Then he remembered: It was her Easter hat, and she'd worn it back when his father lived with them and they still went to church. "Are you going to church, Mom?" he asked. She turned around, and he saw that she'd been crying. For a moment, he was worried that she was going to say something about the windows. But then she said, "While I was in the hospital, I got a letter from Mr. Gilchrist. You remember Mr. Gilchrist, don't you?" Jimmy nodded. Mr. Gilchrist was the vacuum salesman who made the noises with her in the bedroom. "Well, he said he wouldn't be coming to town anymore. He said his company changed his route." She laughed abruptly, then frowned. "Men," she said. She looked at him. "I wish you weren't a boy, Jimmy. You'll grow up to be just like the rest of them, and you'll leave me too."

"No, I won't," Jimmy said.

"Yes, you will."

"No, I won't," he repeated, shaking his head.

"Goddamn it, you will," she said and tore the hat off her head and flung it against the wall. Jimmy flinched and took a step backward. "I'm sorry," she said. "I didn't mean it." She reached out for him. "Come here, honey. I'm sorry."

But he didn't move.

"All right then," she said and dropped her hands to her sides. "Do whatever the hell you want. You will anyway." She got back into bed and pulled the covers up to her chin. Jimmy stood there, watching her. "What are you waiting for?" she said. "Go." And he left.

The next day she was better—she even helped him build a snow fort in the yard until she got too tired—and Jimmy thought everything was going to be all right again. But by mid-January, she was so tired all the time that she had to go back to the hospital. Mrs. McClure said she was a lot better than she had been, but she still wasn't quite well. When Jimmy asked what was wrong with her, she said, "It's nothing to worry about. She just needs a rest." Jimmy tried to convince her that his mother could rest at home—he could clean the house for her and do the laundry and cook—but she only sighed. "It's not just for a rest, Jimmy. Your mother's not very happy right now. At the hospital they'll help her be happy again."

Jimmy didn't say anything then. He knew why she was unhappy; it was all his fault. Why had he thrown those rocks? If he had just put that first rock down and walked away, she wouldn't have to go back to the hospital, and he wouldn't have to go back to the Kahlstroms'. He didn't want to live there anymore. It wasn't that he didn't like the Kahlstroms—he did—but he missed his mother when he was there. Most people didn't know how nice she was; they only saw her when she was too tired to be nice. But sometimes when he'd tell her something funny that happened at school, she'd laugh so hard she'd have to hold her sides, and she'd smile so big there'd be wrinkles around her eyes. He loved that smile, and in the weeks that followed, he often stood in front of the Kahlstroms' bathroom mirror and tried to imitate it. He'd stand there for a long time, smiling at himself with her smile, until Mrs. Kahlstrom would get worried and come looking for him.

*

This time his mother got out of the hospital after only a month, but Mrs. McClure said he couldn't go home just yet. He cried so hard then that the Kahlstroms agreed to let his mother come once a week for a visit. That Sunday Mrs.

McClure dropped her off in her Subaru. Jimmy was upstairs in his room when the doorbell rang. "Your mother's here," Mr. Kahlstrom called, and Jimmy came running downstairs just as he opened the door for her. It was snowing lightly, and her hair and the shoulders of her coat were dusted with snow. "Come on in, Mrs. Holloway," he said and helped her out of her coat. "Welcome to our home."

She didn't look at him. She just cleared her throat and said, "Thank you," then looked at Jimmy, who was standing beside the potted fern in the hall. "Jimmy," she said and knelt on one knee for him to come to her. He had been looking forward to her coming, but now that she was here, he felt strangely shy, and he walked toward her slowly with his eyes down. Then her arms were around him, and she was kissing his cheek. She didn't smell like herself though; she was wearing perfume that smelled like the potpourri Mrs. Kahlstrom kept in an oriental dish in the bathroom. He stepped back and looked at her. Her eyebrows looked darker, and there were red smudges on her cheekbones. As she stood up, her silver earrings swung back and forth. She was smiling, but it wasn't her real smile, the one she gave him when they were alone.

"If you'd like, you can sit in the living room," Mr. Kahlstrom said. "I've just built a fire in the fireplace." He led them to the living room. "I'll leave you two alone," he said and went upstairs to join Mrs. Kahlstrom, who had told Jimmy at breakfast that she hoped he'd understand but she just couldn't be there when his mother came.

Jimmy sat in the wingback chair beside the white brick fireplace and swung his legs back and forth. His mother stood in front of the fire a moment, warming herself and looking at Mrs. Kahlstrom's collection of Hummel figurines on the mantel, then sat down on the end of the sofa next to the chair. He knew he should go sit with her, but he didn't. Then she touched the cushion beside her and said, "Won't you come sit with me?" He nodded and slid out of the chair and climbed up next to her. It felt strange to be alone with his mother in someone else's house—it was like they were actors in a movie or something and not real people. He didn't know what to say to her. He wasn't at all tired, but he stretched and yawned. He didn't know why he'd done that, and he suddenly wanted to be upstairs in his room, playing with his toys, the visit over and his mother on her way back home.

"Mr. Kahlstrom made a fire," he finally said, though she already knew that. Then he added, "He showed me how to do it. First you crumple up newspaper, then you stack up little sticks like a teepee over it and—"

"Jimmy," his mother interrupted. "I wish I could bring you home with me right now. You know that, don't you?"

He nodded.

"It may be a little longer, but I'm going to bring you home with me soon. Okay?"

"Okay," he said.

"And things'll be a lot better than they were last time, I promise. I still had a lot of anger in me then, a lot of hurt. But I don't feel like that anymore. I've got a new outlook, and I'm going to make a better life for us. You'll see."

Jimmy looked at her. "You're not mad anymore?"

"No," she said, and Jimmy smiled. But then she added, "At least not like before. I'm learning to deal with it. It was hard at first, but it's getting easier."

Jimmy looked down then. She was still mad, she still had not forgiven him.

"At any rate," his mother continued, "Mrs. McClure says it won't be long before I can bring you back home."

Then she was silent. She was looking at the flames in the fireplace. One of the logs popped, and some sparks struck the black mesh screen.

Jimmy knew he should say something, but he thought if he opened his mouth, he'd start to cry.

"The Kahlstroms have such a nice house," his mother said then. "I've always loved fireplaces. When I was a girl, I used to imagine the house I'd live in when I got married, and it always had a fireplace in it. And after dinner on cold winter nights, my husband would build a big, roaring fire, and we'd all sit around it and talk, the firelight flickering over our faces." She shook her head and laughed. It didn't sound like her laugh. And the things she was saying didn't sound like anything she'd ever said before. "I had it all figured out," she said. "I was going to have five children. I even had their names picked out—Joseph, Kevin, Abigail, Christine, and John, in that order. No James—that was your father's idea." She laughed again. "I had everything figured out. Every blessed thing." Then she turned her face toward him. There were tears in her eyes. "Don't you ever have everything figured out, you hear? Don't you—"

Then she couldn't talk anymore.

"What's wrong, Mom?" he managed to say.

"I'd better go," she said and stood up. She took a crumpled Kleenex from her purse and wiped her eyes with it. "This was a mistake. I shouldn't be here." She looked around the room at the large-screen TV, the piano, the watercolor landscapes on the walls, the philodendron in the corner, and added, "I don't belong here."

"Don't go," he said, but it was too late. She was already on her way out.

"Tell Mr. and Mrs. Kahlstrom thank you for letting me come see you," she said as she put on her coat.

"Mom," he said. "Mom!"

She leaned over and took his face in her hands and kissed him. "My baby," she said.

And then she was out the door, and he was standing at the window, watching her walk carefully down the icy sidewalk through the falling snow, not even a scarf on her head, and Mr. and Mrs. Kahlstrom were coming down the stairs asking why she had left so soon. When he tried to answer, a sob rose in his throat and stuck. He shook his head, unable to speak.

Mrs. Kahlstrom put her hands on his shoulders. "Don't worry, honey. You'll see her again next week," she said, but he wrenched himself out of her hands and ran upstairs and locked himself in the bathroom. And although Mr. and Mrs. Kahlstrom stood outside the door and tried to comfort him, it was nearly an hour before he came out.

Mrs. Kahlstrom hugged him hard then and said they'd stay downstairs with him next time, if he wanted, so they could make sure his mother wouldn't upset him again. Jimmy didn't say anything for a long moment. Then he took a deep breath and said something he'd been wanting to say for the past four months. "If I get a job delivering papers and save all my money and pay for the windows, will Mrs. McClure let me go back home?"

"Windows?" Mrs. Kahlstrom said, then looked at her husband.

Mr. Kahlstrom wrinkled his forehead. "What windows, Jimmy? What are you talking about?"

And then he confessed it all.

*

Mr. Kahlstrom took Jimmy to see the high school counselor the next afternoon. His name was Mr. Sargent, but he told Jimmy to call him Dale. He was a skinny man with a ponytail, and he was wearing a corduroy sport coat but no tie. He leaned back in his chair and put his scuffed Hush Puppies up on the desk. Behind him, on the wall, was a poster of a strangely dressed black man kneeling in front of a burning guitar. "So, Jimbo," he said, "what's a nice guy like you doing in a place like this?"

Jimmy sat there, looking down at his lap. His hands were shaking, and he couldn't make them stop. He watched them tremble. Somehow it seemed like it was happening a long way away, to somebody else maybe.

"You don't have to be afraid," Mr. Sargent said. "You can say anything in here. This is one place where you can say whatever you want. 'Cause I won't tell anyone anything you say. Everything you tell me will be confidential. And confidential means you can be confident I won't tell anyone your secrets."

Jimmy sat on his hands to make them stop trembling. Then he tried to look up, but he couldn't. Finally he said, "Did Mr. Kahlstrom tell you?"

"Tell me what, Jimbo?" Mr. Sargent said.

Jimmy didn't want to say. He was hoping Mr. Sargent didn't know.

"Tell me what?" Mr. Sargent asked again, more softly this time. "You can tell me."

"The windows," Jimmy managed to whisper.

"Oh, the windows. Sure, he told me about the windows. But who cares about the lousy windows?"

Jimmy looked up, startled. Mr. Sargent smiled and went on. "It was wrong to break the windows, of course, but I don't have to tell you that—you already know it. But once they're broken, there's nothing you can do about it, except admit it like a man and say you're sorry and go on with your life. Everybody makes mistakes. That's how we learn to be better people. If we didn't make mistakes, we'd never learn anything. So think of it that way—as a mistake you made that you can learn from." Here he took his feet down from the desk and leaned forward in his chair. "What have you learned from all of this, Jimbo? Is there anything it's taught you that'll help you on down the road?"

Jimmy didn't think he'd learned anything, unless it was that he wasn't who he'd always thought he was. He didn't know who he was now, but he was someone else. Someone crazy, like his mother. And once Mr. Sargent found that out, he'd make him go to a hospital too.

"Let me guess then," Mr. Sargent said. "You tell me if I'm getting warm, okay?" When Jimmy didn't respond, he repeated, "Okay?" Finally, Jimmy nodded. "All right then. Did you learn that—hmm, let's see—that it's best to talk about your anger instead of breaking things?"

Jimmy hadn't been angry when he broke the windows, but he nodded yes anyway.

"Good. That's a good thing to learn. And did you also learn that secrets make you unhappy? That the longer you keep something inside, the more it hurts?"

Again Jimmy nodded, though he thought he hurt more now that people knew what he had done. And even though Mr. and Mrs. Kahlstrom told him he hadn't been taken away from his mother because he broke the windows, he didn't know if he could believe them. They wanted him to like them, so maybe they would lie. And they wanted to adopt him, so maybe they would tell Mrs. McClure about the windows, and Mrs. McClure would tell his mother, and then she'd say she couldn't take him back because she couldn't afford to pay for the windows like Mr. and Mrs. Kahlstrom could.

"That's good. That's very good. And did you maybe also learn how much people care about you? Because if they didn't, I wouldn't be here talking to you. I'm talking to you because I care and because Mr. and Mrs. K care and because everybody who knows you cares about you and wants you to be happy. Is that maybe something you learned from all of this too?"

Jimmy looked at him, then at the floor. He didn't see the floor, though; he was seeing his father, the morning of the day he left for work and never came back, trimming his mustache in front of the bathroom mirror.

It took him longer this time, but once again he nodded.

*

The following Sunday, Mrs. McClure's Subaru pulled up in front of the Kahlstroms' house, but Jimmy's mother was not in it. "What a terrible day," Mrs. McClure said to the Kahlstroms as she flicked the snow from her boots with her gloves.

"We must have a foot of snow already." Then she cocked her head toward Jimmy. "I'm sorry, sweetie, but your mother isn't feeling well today. She said she'd try to come again next week. I hope you aren't too disappointed."

"You told her, didn't you," Jimmy said.

"Told her what?"

"You know."

"Oh, that. No, I didn't say anything. I told you I wouldn't tell, and I won't." Then she frowned. "Is that why you think she didn't come?"

"You can tell her if you want," he said, sticking his chin out. "She won't come anyway."

"Of course she will. She'll come tomorrow or the day after," Mrs. McClure said. "It's just that today—" But before she could finish, Jimmy turned and started to run up the stairs. "Jimmy!" she called after him. "Let me explain."

At the top of the stairs, he stopped and shouted down, "Tell her I don't care if she ever comes—not ever!" And then he ran into his room and slammed the door.

A few minutes later, he heard Mrs. McClure's car drive away, and then Mr. and Mrs. Kahlstrom came up and tried to talk to him. "We know you were looking forward to seeing her, honey," Mrs. Kahlstrom said, but he just dumped his entire canister of Legos onto the carpet and started putting them together.

"What're you building?" Mr. Kahlstrom asked.

"Nothing," he answered.

"Well," he said, "that shouldn't take much time." But Jimmy didn't laugh. Mr. Kahlstrom cleared his throat and looked at his wife. "Maybe we ought to let Jimmy be alone for a while," he said. Mrs. Kahlstrom nodded and said, "We'll be right downstairs if you need us. Okay, Jimmy?"

Jimmy didn't say anything. And when they left, he got up and closed the door again.

He tried to play with his Legos, but after a few minutes, he gave up and sat on the edge of his bed, looking out the window. It had been snowing all day, and now the snow was so thick he could barely see the houses across the street. He watched the evergreens sway in the yard and listened to the wind whistle in the eaves, then pressed his warm cheek against the windowpane. The window was cold, and it vibrated a little with every gust of wind. It felt as if the glass were shivering, and for a second he thought it might even break. But he didn't move his face away; he pressed his cheek against it harder, until he could feel the cold right through to his cheekbone. He wished he were outside, walking through the waist-high drifts, the wind making his cheeks burn and his eyes tear; he wanted to be so cold that nothing could ever warm him up. That didn't make sense, but Jimmy didn't care if it did or not. He had a lot of thoughts he didn't understand, but he didn't worry about them anymore. You couldn't do anything about the brain that was in your head. Even if you were as rich as Michael Jackson, you still couldn't buy a new brain. You could get a new mother, but you couldn't get a new brain.

*

Later that night Mr. Kahlstrom built a fire, and the three of them sat on the sofa eating popcorn and watching *E.T.* on videotape. The movie was sad, but Mr. and Mrs. Kahlstrom were smiling. It was so easy to make them happy, he thought; all he had to do was sit on the sofa with them. And that thought made him feel bad because he had stayed in his room almost all day, making them worry.

Outside, the snow was still falling, a thick curtain of it, and every now and then the wind would rattle the windowpanes. "My, what a storm," Mrs. Kahlstrom said when the picture on the television flickered and went dark for a second. "We'd better get the candles out."

"It looks like we'll be snowed in tomorrow," Mr. Kahlstrom said. Then he tousled Jimmy's hair. "No school for us, eh, buckaroo?"

Jimmy smiled, and Mrs. Kahlstrom grinned. "I'd like that," she said. "We could sit around the fire and tell stories and play games, the way people did in the olden days. It'd be just like that poem 'Snow-Bound.' I memorized part of it when I was in high school for a talent show." She lowered her head, as if it were immodest of her to say the word *talent*. But then she began to half-speak, half-sing the poem:

What matter how the night behaved?
What matter how . . . the north-wind raved?
Blow high, blow low, not all its snow
Could quench our hearth-fire's ruddy glow.
O Time and Change!—with hair as gray
As was my father's—no, my *sire's*—that winter day,
How strange it seems to still . . .

"No, that's not right," she broke off. "I think I missed a line in there somewhere."

"It sounded great to me," Mr. Kahlstrom said. "Go on. Recite some more for us." And he pressed the pause button on the remote control, freezing E.T. as he raised his glowing fingertip.

"All right," she said, "I'll see what else I can remember." Then she looked toward the ceiling as if the words were above her, floating through the air like snowflakes.

Ah, brother! only I and thou
Are left of all that circle now—
The dear . . . home faces whereupon
That fitful firelight paled and shone.
Henceforward, listen as we will,
The voices of that hearth are still;
Look where we may, the wide earth o'er,
Those lighted faces smile no more . . .

She stopped abruptly and looked down at her lap. Mr. Kahlstrom reached across Jimmy and patted her hand. "It's all right, dear," he said. "Don't cry."

"I'm sorry," she said. "Sometimes I remember and . . ."

"I know, dear. I do too."

Jimmy looked at their faces. He wasn't sure what they were talking about. He hadn't understood the poem either, but he'd liked the way it made him feel warm and cold all at once, as if he had just come out of a blizzard to stand by a fire. He liked the way she'd said it too, pronouncing each word as if it were almost too beautiful to say. And she'd had such a strange look on her face while she said it, kind of sad but in a way happy too. He didn't know how you could be happy and sad at the same time. But now she only looked sad.

Just then the wind rose sharply, and the television went black. The only light left was the firelight. It cast long shadows up the walls around them, making Jimmy feel as if they were in a cave.

"I knew I should have gotten the candles out," Mrs. Kahlstrom said and wiped her eyes.

"Don't worry, dear. I'm sure the electricity will be back on in no time. Let's just sit here and enjoy the fire."

He got up and threw two more logs on, adjusted them with the poker until the flames caught, then sat back on the sofa. "There," he said. "Isn't this cozy?"

They sat together a long time, watching the fire and talking. At first, Jimmy talked too, but after a while he started to grow tired and only listened to their quiet voices and the crackling fire and the wind. The way the wind battered the windows made the fire seem even warmer, and before long, Jimmy felt so drowsy and peaceful that he couldn't help but lean his head against Mrs. Kahlstrom's shoulder. She brushed his hair from his forehead while he listened to them talk and watched the fire through half-open eyes. Finally he couldn't keep his eyes open anymore, and he laid his head down in her lap and fell asleep.

*

When Jimmy woke the next morning, he was confused. It seemed as if only a moment before he'd been lying in front of the fire, and now he was upstairs in his room. How had it happened? Mr. Kahlstrom must have carried him up the steps and put him in his bed, but Jimmy didn't remember it. He felt as if a magician had made him disappear from one place, then reappear somewhere else. For a moment, he wasn't even sure he was the same person. He wondered if his mother had ever felt like that, waking up in the hospital, or if his father had the same thoughts when he sat down for breakfast with his new family. He didn't know, but he lay there a while, thinking about it, before he got up and parted the curtains to look out the window. As far as he could see, everything was white—rooftops, the evergreens and yards, the street. The snow had drifted halfway up frosted picture windows and buried bushes and hedges and even the car parked in the neighbor's driveway. Here and there thin swirls of snow blew into the air like risen ghosts, and sunlight sparked on the drifts, the snow glinting like splintered glass. He'd never seen so much snow, not ever, and he wanted to run to Mr. and Mrs. Kahlstrom's room and tell them they were all snowbound, just like in the poem. But he stood there a while longer and imagined the huge fire they'd build, the yellow and orange flames rising up the chimney, and the three of them sitting beside it, unsure of what to say or even when to speak, but somehow strangely happy, their faces lit by a beautiful light.

Previously published in Black Maps, *University of Massachusetts Press*

DWELLINGS

The hyper-energetic ranger says,
"I doubt you folks know just how lucky you are,
But unlike most dwelling monuments,
We let you go right inside and explore,
We don't hold your hand, we don't
Treat you like you're five years old,
But chewing gum inside the dwellings
Is strictly forbidden, the smell
Attracts insects which may weaken
The structures, and we can't have that,
So if you're chewing, we've got this
Special box. Please deposit your wad
Right here right now. Okay?
You're also lucky because this is
The only region in the country where

You have a chance to see Montezuma quail,
And you could encounter them along the trail.
Montezumas are chunky. They sound like R2-D2 talking,
Followed by the whistle of a small artillery shell."

I ask about the song of the canyon wren,
Which I've hoped to hear for years. "Oh," she smiles,
"I'm-falling-off-a-cliff-and-dying.' Okay?
Everybody ready? I think you're ready. Good luck,
And don't fall off the cliff."

We file up the narrow trail, and it's as if
We're living in a movie from my childhood
About the happy Jesus in the early stage
Of His tragic, short career. Sunlight
Blesses us, the little creek is talking
Like a baby, and resinous perfumes
Haunt the mountain air. We bend
To delight in tiny desert blooms.
We nibble the leaves of herbaceous plants.
We climb. And climb. Our legs burn
'Til we turn at the final switchback and stop.

There they are: the houses of the Mogollon,
The color of ivory, the color of bone,
Set into caves of this half-hid canyon
Off the great valley where the Gila River runs.

White dirt and rock slope away
Toward the chasm. I teeter and shuffle
With care. Would it not be helpful, I think,
If my left leg were just a wee bit shorter than my right?
I worry about my wife, a feckless extravert,
Interested in everything. And our friends,
Who move about with such casual unconcern.
And congratulate myself on my courage, a virtue
They lack since they so clearly feel no fear.

Archaeologists—experts who play seriously
With dirt, who sift through dust and detritus,
Who handle pots gone to pieces, bones,
And teeth as if they were treasure—tell us
The Mogollon arrived from the north
Seven centuries back and holed up here,
Where they felt safe, high on the canyon wall,
Where others had stayed before them,
The Ancient Ones, whose fires had
Already blackened the roofs of the caves,
And before them, the lions, the mountain lions
Who'd gotten in out of the rain and welcomed
This cool retreat from the scorching sun.
Something of their spirit remains,
For we feel ourselves hushed and soften our tones.

The Mogollon arrived from the north

And set these off-white buildings like teeth
In the mouths of the caves. Small, flat stones
Were glued together with mortar made
From dusty tuff. Some walls go right
To the edge and dizzy me so
I can't look. Storerooms still contain
Corn cobs the size of a large man's thumbs.
Pine pole beams penetrate walls
And still hold up the sky.
People lived here. These were their bedrooms,
Windows, walkways. Patios, plazas,
Little piazzas all slant away
Toward the canyon's abyss. People
Lived here. Dwelt. Red pictographs
Remain: a scorpion eats a snake,
A man continues to play his flute.
His music inhabits the wind.

The Mogollon arrived from the north,
Built these houses, dwelt, lived here
One long lifetime, and left. But why?
They were never attacked. Best guess:
A twenty-year drought
Drove them out, back north to vanish
Into the pueblos. Or so the experts
Say, but who doesn't like to speculate,
To guess-and-by-golly? Ron says,

"I think they just got sick of hauling
Water all the way up from the creek."
Sue says, "Too many kids fell off the cliff."

We back down a wooden ladder with care
And cautiously walk the chalky path
That zigzags toward the creek. Birdsong
Showers us—bright and loud—
A cascade of silvery notes that say,
I'm-falling-off-a-cliff-and-dying
Without words, a song sung high to low,
A startling, swift, sweet descent. We look,
Look up! There he is, on the clifftop,
White breast, overlong bill open for song,
As if he were drinking the sky. He flies
To a crack in the rock face, proclaims
His existential aria once more. Again.
Again. With feeling. We can't stop smiling
As we descend, stupidly happy, vaguely stunned
By the sparkling song of the canyon wren.

We are all of us, of course, falling off a cliff
And dying, but let our descent be slow,
And may we sparkle as we go. And could we
Not only live but dwell? I have seen
The stone houses of Ireland, adobe homes

Of New Mexico, the dwellings of the Mogollon.
A poem is also a kind of house
Where we can dwell a while. I built this one
By hand, fit one word next another in rows.
I'm leaving now, but you're welcome. Please.
Make yourself at home. May this house hold,
For you, faint flute music of the desert wind,
Echoes of the wren's annunciation,
And a whiff of mountain lion.

BEDS FOR THE HOMELESS

We pulled the nails from painted wood
And planed it so the grain looked good,

Glued the Douglas fir and pine,
Clamped the pieces over time

'Til they had set, and we could cut
Headboards, legs, and sides to fit.

As we bent to putty holes,
With pampered bodies, troubled souls,

We bowed our heads, as if in prayer,
While saws and joiners tore the air.

Routers carved a fine design
In headboards, keeping you in mind

And how the hover of a dove
Might bless your rest, your making love,

Easing children off to sleep,
Breathing slowly, dreaming deep.

These beds now number sixty-nine:
Two thousand hours of our time.

A land where families freeze in cars
Has wished upon some evil star.

Our sleep is fitful, peace is marred,
Considering this nation's ours.

May these beds support your health.
Forgive us for our luck and wealth.

AN EVENING OF SWEDISH FOLK SONGS

There are bony brown cows in this music,
Mugs of hot milk spiced with pepper.
The last few asters of autumn are here,
The first flickering flakes of snow.
Moonlight is trapped in these tunes,
The cries of white-haired women,
And the wind sneaks in beneath the door.
Here is the breadknife my sister stuck in the landlord's guts,
A Bible, a candle, and a birchbark bowl
In the low-slung hut made of sod and sticks
Where I lived six hundred years ago.

Previously published in Bart Sutter's collection, Nordic Accordion: Poems in a Scandinavian Mood, *Nodin Press, 2018*

Memoir
by Michael Enich

UNPACKING HOME

When I stepped out of Humphrey terminal, I emerged into a crisp Minneapolis fall day—one for which the jean jacket I wore was just barely warm enough. I had my two bags in hand and felt like a pop-up traveler ready to move into whatever space I was offered. My hair was long then; the wind meant I kept compulsively pushing the curls away from my eyes so I could see the cars driving up. Every once in a while, my hand would stay and nervously coil the strands around my finger in one direction, then back in the other, then back in one direction, then back in the other.

My new boss pulled up in a blue Ford Escape, one I would get to know well from our early-morning drives to the hospital. "I almost didn't recognize you with your long hair!" he said through the passenger window. I let out a nervous laugh and hauled my life suitcases into the back of the car. As I settled into the passenger seat by subtly kicking away used paper towels, Sparkling Ice bottles, and the waxy wrappings from mini

Babybel cheeses, I was posed a question. It would be emblematic of my new job as a scribe for this physician, my boss and roommate/host father:

"Hey, I hope you don't mind, but can we stop at the hospital before we go home? I need to take care of some consults."

The "stop" at the hospital morphed into six hours of on-the-job training and took a solid bite out of me settling into my new bedroom, i.e. my boss and his wife's former den. I earnestly laid out my clothes in one of the suitcases on the floor and set my journal on the sofa shelf. As I settled on his couch (for the next four months), I could only have imagined the crash course in this specific world of medicine I would receive. It included my first of many steps to becoming a clinician myself: my first full write-up, my first assertive practice boundaries, my first active choosing of self-care and stepwise self-love. It was the first time I had to learn how to unpack home.

*

I had just come off a year of service in an intentional community. There, I and three other dedicated disciples shared everything. The Peace Corps–style program made sure we had just enough money and resources to get by, amounting to $1 per meal per person per day plus rent and utilities. We were just barely comfortable and learned one another's idiosyncrasies by having deeply personal struggles over seemingly meaningless things—like arguing over whether we should buy bread from the chain grocery store down the street where most people in our neighborhood would go or if we should buy it from the local Cuban bakery, which would mean actively choosing to reinvest in a community that was superficially our own.

At the end of this year, we would sarcastically joke that the process was ultimately a "lesson in failure." I, at least, learned that being intentional was hard. But alongside the guilt of using the Wi-Fi after community hours, or secretive silence of buying a train ticket to visit my boyfriend using my personal savings, or frustration of having to leave a gathering early for community night was a sense of pride. I was proud of letting our neighbor use our driveway for a car repair business, of marching in a protest and having the young people experiencing homelessness I worked with join me, and of developing a college access program more or less on my own.

I cannot imagine something more opposite of intentional community than living in your boss's man cave. Nothing about dwelling in the basement of a house perched on a lake with a sprawling four-mile path around it (not to mention being afraid to use the kitchen because of the three cats you're allergic to) said "home" after a year of shared meals in an intentional community with three like-minded millennials serving specific groups of vulnerable people. It was an unexpected whiplash that foreshadowed a challenging year.

*

My job with this socially acceptable cult was at a crisis shelter for eighteen- to twenty-one-year-olds. My basement experience loosely echoed the experiences of the young people using our beds. I have always struggled to summarize what my year as a youth advocate/education assistant meant on a broader scale. In short, I learned that young people can easily become homeless because of how intersectional the problem of youth homelessness is. Each aspect of their identity provided an unfortunate opportunity that led them to the crisis shelter door; jumping a turnstile because you had no money to get to your therapy appointment meant a ticket you couldn't pay, for example. After that came the warrant, then being kicked out of your family home after being arrested. From a strength perspective though, each portion of these people's identity presented as a potential space for intervention as well; a few people were attending college despite existing in our transitional system.

I shared identities with a few young people, and they tended to strike me most deeply. Queer young people made me wonder what my life would have looked like if my parents had kicked me out of the house when I came out to them. Clients with a mental illness made me wonder about how my own struggle with mental health could have morphed into something different than it was. I pondered this most when my anxiety disorder intermittently and inexplicably reared its ugly head.

*

FI started my work as a psychiatric scribe with vigor. I was grateful for an immediate employment opportunity during which I could go to medical school interviews. At least in this role, I wouldn't have to lie about vacation days or say I would be interested in a case manager position for "two to three years" before "determining what the next step in my career would be."

However, working on an inpatient, double-locked psychiatric unit was difficult for many reasons. My job was to sit in endless interviews but not participate—the skills I had built in talking to young people were lost to typing silently in an exam room. I bore witness to many evaluations, people at what was probably one of the lowest points of their life. I was to do nothing more than type out the transaction for ease of documentation on the psychiatrist's behalf.

I also struggled with panic disorder, a type of anxiety disorder centered around perpetual fear of having unexpected, out-of-the-blue panic attacks. Classically, a person is afraid to leave their home because out there, in the world, they could be struck with sudden anxiety that would debilitate them in public. For a period of time, I was this picture. Somehow, almost miraculously, I had overcome that specific fear to have it replaced with an omnipresent, lingering thought that would spin like a pinwheel—"I could have a panic attack now or now or now or now…" Some days it was easier to ignore the spinning than others.

I found it hard to just listen as a scribe with this glittery distraction in the back of my head. It felt like chance that I had never sought so badly to escape my anxiety that the only solution seemed to be ending my life. This sentiment echoed similarly to these aspects of my identity—being gay, experiencing a mental illness—never precariously sliding me into me being housing unstable. Day by day, feeling restricted without any autonomy in my host family's basement, sharing a bathroom with my boss, riding in the same car at 6:15 in the morning, I came closer and closer to truly understanding the liminal space my young people went through every day, potentially for years on end.

This discomfort continued to rear its head in ugly ways and lingered for a year afterward. I couldn't ride for long periods in the car out of fear I would have a panic attack, have to reveal that aspect of my identity to my boss, and have to pull over to the side of the highway to catch my breath. This made driving the psychiatrist to speaking engagements hard, made flying home to Chicago hard, and made riding the train once I was home hard. I would feel trapped in the small exam rooms; I couldn't really handle driving on my own out of an irrational fear I would somehow crash. I would feel my heart pick up speed at the dinner table with new people I didn't know or on the phone with pharmacies. There seemed to be no safe corner for my mind to wander into. I found myself counting down the days until I could finish the job and move onto the next phase of my life, medical school.

One time while driving the doc to a networking event for alumni of our college (where I had met him two years before), out of the blue he asked "Are you doing okay?" I had already spent forty-five minutes of the drive watching the pinwheel spin in my head and suddenly felt as though someone else could see it too. In that moment of shared understanding, I was able to tell him just how anxious I had been—how having an anxiety disorder that had contributed to one of the darkest moments in my life made it hard for me to watch and document, sometimes word for word, the darkest part of others'. "I spend my day swimming in 'what if's,'" I said, "thinking I just as easily could have ended up on a psych unit." What if I had? What if I did?

As we climbed out of the car, he reminded me that I was doing a good job. Somehow through the chaos of days full of consults, I had lost sight that he was paying attention to the work I was doing. He was reading my notes! And somehow, in the process, I had learned about psychiatric illness and in-advertently improved my ability to document and understand a medical assessment—a skill that would put me ahead of my peers at school a year later. Though challenging, through that conversation I realized that I could simultaneously struggle with my thoughts and succeed at my job; I could be uncomfortable in a house but find home on a couch in the den, watching *Project Runway* and eating hummus after a run.

But within this dissonance I could peer into the world of homelessness more than I ever expected to. I was *not* homeless, obviously, or even housing unstable and was more comfortable than my young people could have dreamed of. I experienced perpetual unease though, outside the context of a quirky but incredibly supportive community I had left behind. I could flex my empathic imagination and understand with new insight their experience; my basic needs were being met but a pervasive unease infiltrated what I did from day to day. It made me think of our young people who each carried their parcel of burden over their shoulder—the one who sat through my incredibly dull GED classes, despite getting in a fight with the person they were sitting next to; the one experiencing hallucinations while listening to guest lawyers answer legal questions; the one who had to take the long way back from high school so their friends wouldn't see they were homeless. Feeling "homeless" was symbolically about never having the comfort to unpack this parcel, to reveal its intricate workings the way my boss had allowed me to do on the ride to the networking event.

*

I eventually moved out. It was not until I laid in my own bed that I realized home was a physical as well as a mental construct. Of course, I appreciated a quiet space without fear of running into my boss—especially because I wouldn't have to share a bathroom. I am grateful that I was able to move in with two people who supported my new early-morning commute out of the city, watched *Grey's Anatomy*, and tolerated my small anxieties. The small moments of panic still lingered, but having my own place meant the stoic observer guise was off for a few hours each day. Lowering the charade meant lowering my guard enough for the panic to subside; it meant starting to unpack my psychic parcel to understand what made it tick in the first place.

Four years later, I sit on my bed in my large and comfortable apartment halfway across the country. I am a medical student now, slamming down words to convey the ongoing journey of building a home away from my comfort in Minneapolis. I finished my psychiatry clerkship, and I felt the tug on my shoulder picking up the work again. Every day I bundled insecurities that I had worked for so long to lay out for my inspection. I felt the weight, and I brought it to my work again—feeling the panic on the hour-long highway commute, the claustrophobia of listening to someone else speak in exam rooms. This time, though, I could present this understanding to patients—recognize their shared burden and attempt to unwrap it with them. Our implicit shared understanding hopefully allowed us both to recover as I talked familiarly about panic attacks or without judgment when a woman said she exchanged sex for a place to stay.

The process of homesteading is long and enduring with some setbacks. Let this be the quiet manifesto to the duty of unpacking them over and over again, a little more completely each time.

BALLAD OF THE ARTHUR AND
EDITH LEE HOUSE

Like an itty-bitty dollhouse.
Made of pretty, white wood.
Happy green grass in front and back.
Cozy and still it stood.

Some say it came right out the box.
Right off a train from Sears.
It came from heaven, Mama sang,
An answer to our prayers.

Papa checked the basement and roof.
The windows, doors, and stairs.
Then he nodded his head and winked,
Mama's eyes bright with tears.

We came in a big friendly truck.
Truck full of old and new.
Beds, chairs, tables, lamps, and dishes.
We thought the sky smiled blue.

That night we heard a far rumble.
We thought it came from dreams.
Next morning flung at our doorstep:
"Get out!" "No colored!" Screams.

"Fighting in France, who moved me out the mud?
"I will make this house my home," Papa said.

All day the sidewalk grumbled
A storm up from the ground
Building a wall of angry fear
White faces all around.

Somebody said, "Think of your kid.
And wife. Let's make a deal."
Hundreds more cash—than Papa paid.
"Our buy-back price, your steal."

All night the neighborhood trembled
Earthquake's defiant fear.
Next day the crowd swelled like a flood.
Not one cop, far and near.

"Colored boy don't want our buy-back?
Where's the government?"
Somebody picked up mud and rocks.
Somebody, excrement.

Inside we huddled with friends.
Our first lawyer talked and talked.
Upon our lawn, up three front steps
The loud mob walked and gawked.

"Nobody moves me out. Alive or dead.
Not at war in France. Not home," Papa said.

Who called again law and order?
"No! Burn it down! It's done!"
"Let's make a deal" somebody said.
Lord! Who said, "Here's my gun"?

Round and round, back and forth, the mob
Blazed and sputtered for days.
The world deaf, dumb, and blind because
The press shuttered its gaze.

Then on the 15th of July
The press uncorked that choke.
Home Stoned in Race Row! Mob Mauls Cop!
The gates of hell just broke.

Three Thousand Renew Their Attack!
From miles and miles they came
Like a lynching or a witch burning
Clogging streets without shame.

Then a prim Amazon of the law
Hammered her gavel down.
"My client has nothing to trade,
Barter, or sell. It's done."

"I have a right to establish a home," Papa said.
What Papa said, he did. Yes, he did. Yes, he did.

What Papa said, he did.

* The Arthur & Edith Lee House at 4600 Columbus Avenue South, Minneapolis, Minnesota, was the center of an urban riot in the summer of 1931. The Lee family stayed in their home until the autumn of 1933. During that time, they slept in the basement, and their daughter Mary was escorted to kindergarten by the police. Their house is on the National Register of Historic Places as is the home of their attorney, Lena Olive Smith, a female pioneer of African-American civil rights.

FALLING FORWARD

You see, there are all those early memories; one cannot get another set; one has but those. –Willa Cather, SHADOWS ON THE ROCK

All my early memories are of my childhood home in St. Paul, Minnesota, the place where we lived for three years and then left, oh so suddenly, when my father decided that some foam rubber he was working on was making him sick. He needed to be in a place where he could work out of doors, he said, where he could breathe clean air and not be poisoned. So he moved us to California, to the place that Beat poet Lew Welch described as "the final cliffs of all man's wanderings"— to Santa Barbara, which is a paradise by anyone's standards, but not to me, not then. I didn't understand it this way at age eleven, but later I would come to realize that, in this life of limited symbols, a life in which we may all have one story to tell, Minnesota was to be my paradise, and California my East of Eden.

*

When I remember that paradise—Minnesota in the 1950s—I think first of our house, which looked exactly like the houses you see in storybooks. Yellow with bluish trim, it stood three stories high, and its narrow side faced the street. Being so tall and narrow, it whispered concealment and mystery. At the same time, it beckoned, with a zinnia-filled window box and blue hydrangea bushes ranged along the front wall. Its door was arched with a round window in it, like a hobbit's hole, and surrounded by a latticework forming a small portico.

The inside of the house harbored secret apertures that my sisters and I felt were known only to us, the initiates. A laundry chute traversed the distance between the second floor and the basement. Its metal sides echoed when we shouted "Witch!" to tease our mother as she washed the clothes. In my bedroom was another mysterious opening—this one in the floor, designed as a primitive fire escape; through it I could save my life in a conflagration by dropping into the closet of the room below. My father had camouflaged the unsightly hole with a table, but I considered it one of the special features of my room and delighted in showing it off to visitors.

*

It was, of course, my room that I loved best. My father had made it for me in the attic, cleverly fashioning wood-paneled walls with brass latches that could be opened to retrieve stored objects behind them, and building in the essential furniture, including a desk made from a door. My mother likewise had put her stamp on the room, sewing a bedspread in an aqua cotton print with a ruffled pillow sham to match. She painted my small black hope chest and gave me a booklet with a pink cover called "How to Have a Prettier Room." This booklet provided a system for identifying your personality type— Tomboy, Classic, or Romantic. I was planning to be a Romantic and decorate my room accordingly.

My father transformed our backyard into a wooden playground. Between the house and the dusty alley, he built a monkey bars, adapting it from an old oak ladder, which he swathed in shiny yellow and blue tape to prevent splinters. For acrobatic stunts, he erected two freestanding bars at different heights; they straddled the space between the crab apple tree and the yellow locust. My friend Mary Lou and I would crouch on the bars, callused hands tightly gripping, hesitant. Then my father would come out and exhort us: "Fall forward!" he would say. "Fall forward and you won't get hurt!" Our courage barely edging out our fear, we would lean forward until our bodies swung around and hung upside down under the bars; then we would skin the cat and land safely on the ground.

My father hung two swings in our yard—one from the branches of the yellow locust tree, for standing and pumping; and the other from the rotating metal clothesline, for sitting and singing. I sat there swinging by the hour, dragging my feet in the dust as I sang: "Swing high, swing low, upon a trapeze" and "There's a wideness in God's mercy like the wideness of the sea."

*

Twenty-five children lived on our block, so I rarely felt the want of a playmate. Often, on hot summer days, we would play

War and Old Maid on the Sinicos' front porch or drape blankets over a card table to make a shady fort. Other times we would form two lines in the street, taking baby steps and giant steps in Mother May I? or crashing into the arms of the opposing team in Red Rover, Red Rover. My favorite game was Free the Bunch, a variation on Hide-and-Seek in which the last person who makes it safely back to the base can liberate everyone who has been caught. I loved every aspect of that game: the peacefulness of hiding, the thrill of running as fast as I could to the base, and the cheers of the captives when I succeeded in freeing them all. At the end of the day, my mother might let us take our plates of food to the rock near Hamline Avenue. Trapezoidal with a flat top, the rock was big enough for three small girls to sit side by side and eat their suppers. We named it "Sam" for Susan, Ann, and Martha.

In winter, we would take our red and blue sleds and go sledding down Tarzan Hill or go ice skating at Edgecomb Rink. I still remember the feel of the sled's smooth wooden rudder in my hands as I steered it faster and faster down the slope, and the novel sensation of skating backwards, zigzagging on the ice. "I'm really getting good at this!" I remember thinking the winter before we moved away.

Even before the end of our time in Minnesota, there were signs of what was coming.

A few months before we left, my father, an inventor at Minnesota Mining and Manufacturing Company (3M), quit going to work and stayed in his bedroom with the windows open in the dead of winter. My mother carried his meals to him there and washed the slipcovers over and over to get rid of the poison he thought was in them. In the spring, my father went away for a while, driving to California, coming back, and leaving again. When he returned the second time, it was announced that we would be moving at the end of summer.

*

Moving was already a way of life with us; we had lived in seven different homes by the time I was eight and had made several dramatic relocations—from Little Rock, Arkansas, to New York City; from Long Island to a Pennsylvania dairy farm; and from Ridgewood, New Jersey, to St. Paul, Minnesota. My parents were ambitious, and like many Americans, they equated moving up with moving on. As my mother said in one of her early letters to her parents: "I'm sure we are really going places and everything will be perfect." But this last uprooting was to be different for me and, I now believe, different for my father too.

All our previous moves had been designed, ostensibly, to foster his career. The move to Minnesota reflected a promotion to "Idea Man," a reward from 3M for my father's one great success as an inventor. He had invented the Magic Bow Machine, which makes the pompons with all the loops that you see on Christmas and birthday presents. Our move to California, by contrast with the earlier moves, was inspired by a fear of danger in the place we were in, not a dream of success in the place we were going to. In fact, my father had no job in California at the time we moved there. When he did find work, it was as a salesman for a pharmaceutical company. He would have many jobs in sales during his lifetime. Unlike the job at 3M, however, none was on the path he had set for himself when, in high school, he embarked on a quest for fame and fortune.

I did not fare well in beautiful California. I appreciated the flowering plants—the hibiscus, fuchsia, and bougainvillea—and the hummingbirds, unknown in Minnesota. Nonetheless, I developed symptoms. I lost my independence, became afraid to go to school, the movies, church, anywhere. Every morning on the way to the bus stop, I vomited on purpose to ward off further ills.

*

At that time, I saw no end to my fears. I remember thinking, "I'll never be able to go to the dances like the big girls." But as the years passed, my symptoms lessened, or rather, they took a more acceptable form: that of compulsive study and avoidance of human relationships. I came to love social studies, especially world geography, with its exotic-sounding places such as tundra and steppes. I spent hour after hour learning the beautiful Spanish language, becoming a fourteen-year-old expert on the imperfect subjunctive, the form of "might have been." Years later, thumbing through my old Spanish workbook, with the picture of Don Quixote on its golden cover, I saw, at the top of one page, a heading as familiar as a favorite doll: "Use the Subjunctive with Verbs of Desiring, Wanting, Preferring. Desear, Querer, Preferir."

In time, I graduated valedictorian of Santa Barbara Junior and Senior High Schools, went on through Occidental College, and embarked on a master's degree in Latin American studies at Columbia University. Throughout these years, I rarely looked back. The only sign of my undiminished love of Minnesota was my unfailingly joyous response to cold weather and snow. Then, when I was nearing the end of my first year in graduate school, my father—who by then had spent time in a mental hospital and been diagnosed as paranoid—shot himself in the head one April morning.

I once heard a celebrity reply to the question, posed by a journalist, "How did your father's death affect you?" His answer could serve for me as well: "I came to." As horrible as it was, the tragedy transformed me. I became less bookish and turned outward to people again. In a psychoanalytic textbook years later, I found a name for what had happened: traumatic cure.

*

In my fortieth year of life, I awakened early one morning out of a dream. In this dream, I was back in Minnesota gliding on the ice. When I woke up, a great sadness came over me as I remembered Minnesota and all I had left behind. I felt so strongly that the move was a break, a change that could never be undone. And I thought to myself: I have never even been back.

*

I had booked a room at the only place to stay in our old neighborhood, a rather shabby motel on a highway with construction going on, and I wondered whether I would not have been better off staying in the St. Paul Hotel downtown. Frances, a former neighbor who still lived on our block, had volunteered to pick me up and show me around. At my request, she drove me first to the rock named Sam. Wanting to be alone, I asked if I could get out and walk to the house from there. I went over and embraced the rock as an old friend.

I walked up the street to our house. Everything looked the same as in the pictures I had taken with my Brownie camera; there was the Junkels' H-shaped driveway, where we used to roller skate; the Sinicos' screened-in porch, where we had played cards; and Rabbi Plaut's elegant white house, where I had gone many times to borrow the Oz books. Frances thought it would be all right to unlatch the gate and enter the backyard of our house. It, too, was just the same, if a bit smaller than I remembered. Suddenly I understood why I had put off my return for so long. It was unbearable to think of the life I might have lived and had not, no longer could. Frances took pictures of me standing by our house; I am unsmiling and somber.

*

That evening, in a Japanese restaurant, Frances and her husband, Frank, told me their recollections of my father: "We loved your dad," said Frances. "We thought he was brilliant."

"He was a very bright, imaginative, witty fellow," Frank said. "I always had a feeling he could do anything he wanted to do; with all that talent, it's just too damned bad." They wanted to know more about the end of his life. I started to describe how my father had lived alone in a shack with a shotgun in a corner and rats running freely through the rooms, but I became upset and left most of my dinner uneaten.

As we left the restaurant, daylight still lingered in the sky, and we drove to my old house, where Frances had arranged for me to meet the current owners. When we arrived, I was taken on a tour by the owners' children: nine-year-old Michael and five-year-old Shelby, as well as Muffin, their fat calico cat.

Michael and I hit it off instantly, chatting like old friends about the quirks of the house and my attic bedroom, which was now his. Upon reaching the second floor, I excitedly predicted the location of the laundry chute; it had been painted over, but was still visible. As we stood looking at it, I said, "The place I really want to see is up there," and started up the steep attic steps with Michael and Shelby following.

*

The room had not changed; there were the same sharply inclined walls with knotty pine paneling, the same ceiling that was only five feet wide at its level part, the same bannister and built-in bookcase, now rather dilapidated. The hole in my bedroom floor was still there, and Michael lifted the table to show me just as I had done with my visitors some thirty years before. We sat on Michael's bed, and I looked around at the pictures of teenage athletes that now adorned the walls. Suddenly, my eyes spotted something familiar. Rising, I walked to the closet, where I seemed to recognize the pounded copper pull on the door. On closer inspection, I was sure: It was the same pull that had been there when I was a child; certainly it was ancient, for one side of the crescent-shaped pull had come off the door and was hanging down. I curled my fingers around the cool metal and said, "My father put this here. The last time I touched this pull, I was eleven years old."

After a while we trooped down to the basement; it had been refinished since the days when my mother, as the witch doing laundry, listened to our echoing cries. Shelby picked up a long rope with red handles. "Do you want to play jump rope?" she asked.

"Yes," I said gaily, moving between the two children. "Not last night/ But the night before/ Twenty-four robbers came/ Knocking at my door . . ." I jumped toward the twirling rope.

Previously published under the title "Return to Eden" in Passages North, *vol. 23, no. 1, Winter/Spring 2002*

WINTER HEART

Elle was happily driving us around because she knew what the reward waiting for us would be once we found a good parking spot. Her face was glaring with her typical sly smile, the smile of someone who is up to no good but having fun while doing it. She picked up her vape and inhaled it solemnly, as if that puff were the last one she was going to take in a while, and exhaled a sweet-smelling cloud of chemically processed nicotine juice, flooding the car with a thick white cloud, making it look like an intoxicating steam room. Every time after that, if I got even a faint whiff of a similar smell on the street, it would trigger memories of her, of this night, and of all the other nights we were looking for a good parking spot.

We finally found a poorly lit parking lot in front of a city park, but we noticed an empty car already parked there, warning us of other humans roaming around. As we carved a space into a parking slot, the headlights of another car entering the lot flooded our illicit intentions. *Shit.* Finding a good spot in a residential area was much harder than I had originally thought.

It had never crossed my mind that residential areas are well lit, packed with people, without many parks or big empty lots. We were looking for a place inconspicuous enough because we were in no mood to have an evening chat with a police officer. I had almost started to lose my motivation when Elle pulled me out of my mental rut with a squeeze to my forearm.

"I know where to go!" she said all bubbly. I loved the feeling of her hand grabbing mine with that firm squeeze, perfectly conveying her excitement with the exact amount of tactile energy. "Let's go to the top of a parking ramp. Nobody should be parked there at this time."

Her idea was brilliant. This is why I loved her. She could conjure the cleverest solutions to the silliest little problems you never thought you would find yourself in. She was six years younger than me, but her mind was a million light years ahead of mine. When I was twenty years old, I felt like I could barely wipe my own ass; but in her twenties, she could keep her whole family afloat.

"I know exactly where that is," I replied immediately. I was able to picture the place she was thinking about because I had parked there innumerable times at points during the day when people were hustling to their appointments.

When we arrived, the only thing we could see around us was the snow freely drifting and dancing in waves across the concrete, making little snow banks. The sight was bone-chilling in and of itself, but not for us, since a four-story parking lot in a residential area—where most buildings were two stories high at most—meant we were gods in that level, in our own little kingdom. Also, after several years of living in this inclement weather, I had finally learned to embrace it. It is weird how easily you forget what used to be normal once you change your context. Every winter I spent in Minnesota, I would learn something new. Back where I'm from, we weren't strangers to cold weather, but subzero Celsius temperatures in that latitude of South America was a memorable once-a-year event. It snowed maybe twice a year in the city; snow was something that belonged more on the mountains. Here in Minneapolis, I figured out by the second year of almost complete hibernation that smoking pot and watching TV all winter long was going to make me suicidal, so I had to adapt to my new home one clothing layer at a time. By now, enjoying winter while avoiding frostbite was second nature.

I looked at the temperature reading on the car dashboard: 10 degrees Fahrenheit. I knew this was my comfort temperature to go outside and hike for an hour or more, provided I had good clothing, but I was not sure how being semi naked in a car would feel at such a temperature, even with the heater blasting. This was new and exciting. Plus, the rush of doing something on the border of legality always heightens anything you do, even if you have done it a thousand times.

That was probably the reason why I fell in love with her. Elle was a partner in crime. Our mischievousness resonated at the same wavelength. We didn't just complement each other. We exponentiated each other. We wanted to constantly outdo each other, to relentlessly outsmart each other, but always with each other. I wished for that moment we could always be together, living the happy ending of a romantic comedy, sitting on a bench overlooking the sea, being old, talking about this and many other adventures, but life wasn't a romantic comedy; if anything, it's a comedy of ironies randomly thrown at you.

"What are you thinking about?" she said

"Nothing," I quickly replied with the tone of a child hiding a secret.

"C'mon," she said. She raised her eyebrows.

"I don't kno—"

"What was your last thought?" She had a way of prying out any thought I had, which is why she would hear my darkest thoughts, never seeming afraid of any of them. She could make me feel vulnerable and comforted in one big swoop.

"I was just thinking about how I don't really miss much of where I grew up, probably because I forget things quickly, and I was wondering if I would forget this moment, and if we—"

"Don't overthink it. We are right where we want to be right now," she said.

"I know I am, Elle, but you know it's very likely someone is going to get hurt eventually," I said.

"We can stop before that happens," she said.

We never did. It was naive to think you can stop fast-developing feelings, but when you are right in the middle of them, it seems like you can catch them easily, even though there is nothing more elusive than trying to catch a feeling you willingly gave into. By the time you are done, you realize you were trying to catch a tornado, and you are not sure if the mess left is from you frantically trying to catch something that you couldn't possibly contain or from the cataclysmic event itself that could have been avoided. When you open the door to such seductive feelings, your mind makes sure to justify any consequence, covering up any guilt with lust. Maybe in the end I actually wanted all the nasty consequences; maybe it was a life crisis to which I needed the right catalyst, and she was the perfect one.

"Will we?" I asked.

"I hope so, Enrique. I mean, even though I do like hanging out with you," She said.

"Hanging out?"

"Well, hanging out with perks," she replied.

I laughed. "You call this perks?"

"Oh, are they not?" she shot back at me.

"Well, if the perks that you get in stores were like the perks I'm getting here, there would be a lot of really happy people," I said.

"And a lot of conflicted people," she answered.

"Indeed," I said. I smiled at her cheeky comment.

And just like that, I signed my fate. She took another long drag from her vape. This time when she exhaled, I loved the visual effect the cloud made in the car against the parking lights, slightly dimmed, diffused, like we were in the middle of a dance club. The cloud lingered, hanging onto the sexual tension that had been building for the last half-hour. Maybe the dryness of the winter air added static to the situation because the atmosphere around us literally felt charged, ready to spark at any time, oversaturated with the mental images that were being projected into that smoke, dancing, swirling, and mixing up, foretelling what was going to happen within these 20 cubic feet. We looked at each other for a while without doing anything, visually exploring every crevasse and imperfection of our faces before our skin made any kind of contact. We joked that when we blinked while looking at each other, we were actually activating the shutter of our brain, recording mental pictures of each other, trying to imprint into our fragile memories each fleeting moment together.

When we finally started making out, it felt as if we were the discharge, the conductive element as well as the current itself, the physical conduit and the ethereal connection, some kind of nuclear force in infinite combustion, an ever-irradiating source of energy, chaos and serenity dancing a harmonious dance in a never-ending contest to see what the other one would come up with next. Her skin wasn't the softest I had ever touched, nor did she have the best curves I had ever seen, but I didn't care about any of that. Being with Elle felt like dancing salsa effortlessly when you know you are not that good at it; it felt like dribbling a ball against three people and passing them effortlessly, although you suck at sports; it felt like shooting a bow and grouping five arrows in a quarter-sized circle from 50 yards away. It was simple, it was raw, it was unfiltered, it was being in the zone, it was not knowing what time it was and not caring, it was knowing we were doing something forbidden and not caring. It was making love, in a car, in a parking lot, in 10-degree weather, seminaked, on a weekday, and feeling like performing that single act of rebelliousness meant during that precise moment, however ephemeral, we were accomplices of a past lifetime reuniting and reclaiming what rightfully belonged to us. I looked up at her face and remembered how much I liked her loose hair hanging over me and covering both our faces, like a cocoon encapsulating our connection, our small fort of naiveté. I was staring into her soul and trying to record that precise moment in my mind. *Blink.*

"Mental note: Height of the place does matter when making love" I said after we were done, to break the awkwardness of her head constantly bumping the roof of the car when going at it. Having sex in the back of a car on a blanket was awkward, and it definitely was not our best performance, but we didn't care because we were savoring the moment fully and slowly, trying to taste all the flavors contained in each of our kisses. She busted out laughing. In my head her laughter was in slow motion, showing all her imperfect, semicrooked teeth, with the melody of her laughter comparable to a song you obsess over so much you want to have it on repeat for several days. This is when I knew I was already too far into her to stop it from becoming my demise, but I had already decided to deny it so we could keep enjoying each other. I knew I was in love, but I couldn't say it because it was too soon. Up to this day I'm still not sure at which point you are supposed to say you love someone if you feel the connection right away. She noticed I was mentally gone for a little bit longer than usual and asked me what I was thinking about.

"I hate you," I said while staring into her pupils. She smiled. She knew exactly what I meant. There was a small silence while she stared right back at me.

"I hate you too," she mouthed, still smiling, acknowledging she was too far into it as well. With that phrase, we signed a contract to ignore the fact that this was more than a fling, burying it from our conscious so we could keep seeing each other. From that moment on, that would be our little phrase to express our love for each other. *Blink. Blink.*

The windows were completely fogged. Now that the inside of the car was quieter, we could hear the wind gusts shaking the car. We had to get going, we both had to get home. Somehow this car felt more like home than my own home. I thought of the lyrics, "Home is wherever I'm with you." Just then I fully understood the meaning of the phrase. Of course it was.

It wasn't about the material stuff or the physical or a place. It was about the experience, the experience of living, of being alive, of feeling alive, of feeling like you are discovering something new and enjoying that process, like a kid enjoying that exact moment, no matter where it may lead, because an end result was not the point. The point was the experience.

On our drive back, we listened to music and laughed about nothing and everything like we always did. We parked about a block from my place, around the corner. I was dreading going back home.

"Thank you," I said.

"For what?" she replied, smiling, half-surprised.

"For making me feel like a kid again." She smiled and looked at me the way girls look at puppies, but without uttering a sound, trying to contain herself. Her gaze briefly looked away, but when it came back to my eyes, it seemed distant, melancholic.

"I don't want you to go," she said almost pleadingly.

"Me neither," I whispered, feeling something between hopeful and excited with sprinkles of hopelessness. "Is it weird I don't want to go home?"

"There must be a reason for that," she said, giving me an inquiring look.

"I was happy until I met you," I replied, smiling and shaking my head, trying to sound as mean as I could. It didn't sound mean at all.

"Were you?" she said, smiling. That question was, in a way, more hurtful than my comment. She had made me realize that something was missing in my life. Just as when I would visit my country after I moved to Minnesota and recognize that it didn't feel like home anymore, I now knew that my home in Minneapolis was not quite my home anymore.

"I hate you," I said. I stared at her with a mix of love and disappointment.

"I hate you too," she whispered as I opened the car door.

I felt my stomach drop and walked away from the car without looking back.

The hardest part wasn't that I couldn't invite her in. It wasn't that I could not tell her I loved her. It was the change of personalities; it was painfully putting on layers of filters again while walking back home after having previously dropped them like a heavy coat soaked in sleet. It was the shedding of all the infatuation, going also through layers of guilt, and then returning to loving mode, but as a different person. It was like mourning a separation and bouncing back from that grief in the amount of time it takes to walk one block. It was that I repeatedly went through that sadomasochistic process of my own will and I couldn't figure out how to make it stop without shattering everything in hopes of being able to make something better out of the salvageable pieces. It was accepting that making these choices would make me the villain of my own life story and I didn't know if I would ever get a shot at redemption. It was that I needed to feel alive, and in such pursuit, I somehow felt a little bit deader inside. It was not knowing what home was anymore, although in this very moment, I was headed straight toward it.

When I finally arrived at the door, I shuffled through my backpack to find my keys buried in the bottom, and as I opened the door, I felt the warmth and coziness emanating from the apartment.

"Hi, honey!" my wife said.

"Hi, babe," I said. I felt exhausted.

I was home. Again.

BRUEGGERS

I could live in this coffee shop.

The toddler with pulled-up shirt
rubs his round belly,
performs a fat-bottomed downward dog,
takes a gentle tumble,
laughs and runs to the end
of his mother's tether.

I could befriend everyone here—
the jostling soccer team,
the texting girls,
the boy who leans back into the dad
teaching him to speak football,
madonna with the newborn,

tired face alight.

I love families that hug.
Even the teenage girl and her father
whose magnets are
currently set on repel,
a different kind of hug.

There are cafes
in Budapest and Paris
where glossy people
down shots of thick espresso
and opine in glittering phrases.
I might feel smug if I were them.

But I don't live in a sparkling city.
I live where little boys
express themselves in toddler yoga,
skinny teenage boys flaunt
their numbered jerseys
and fathers with round bellies,
their shirts pulled firmly down,
meet my eyes and smile.

Poetry
by Jayson Iwen

SUNRISE

I live with my real dad in a trailer park

on a ridge above town,

and Mom's already on her third husband

over in Wisconsin now.

I had a big brother for a while,

from Mom's first marriage Out West,

but he went to Iraq, and only half of him came back.

Sometimes I feel like I'm the other half,

haunting his old life,

but that's usually nights when Dad's on the road,

and I'm alone, and to make the feeling go away

I curl up with Tiger on the couch,

and we watch war movies in the dark,

and I smoke Dad's cigarettes.

Mom was drunk at the funeral,

moaning and crying things like
"My baby is dead!" and "I love him more than anyone else!"
and "Why did God do this to me!"
She left early to get more drunk,
and everyone was relieved to see her go.
I don't hate her. I know that Out West
was some kind of Eden for her,
and she burned it down in grand style,
and she thought she could get away from it,
but it's burning inside her still,
and she drinks to put it out,
but that only feeds the fire.
I suppose you could say she's in hell.
And I'm just across the river.
Sometimes I sit outside on the steps
and imagine Travis sitting beside me.
"You shouldn't be smoking," he says.
"You shouldn't be dead," I say.
"Everyone dies," he says. "It's natural as the sunrise."
"What does it feel like?"
"Like coming home from far away."

Roze & Blud, the manuscript from which "Sunrise" was excerpted, was the winner of the 2020 Miller Williams Poetry Prize, University of Arkansas Press.

WITH THE HARD BAND ROCKING OFF
FOR THE WEEKEND

I stayed alone at the house on Crime Street,

in an expansive time drawn out and drummed in

by the riddle of how I'd wound up in such a dump.

Contracting floorboards had formed pyramids,

which loomed larger than the sum of their boards.

Too high to step over, we had to walk around them.

In our kitchen with its vast pyramid and congested

traffic pattern, we were eight rowdies pushing our way

around, each of us in turnraising a chicken leg in jest,

to beat the others back. But on the weekend—

with all the bravado gone—I was alone, matching wits

with midnight, for l was too alert, too there,

ears open to every door. I had developed a mild case

of omnipresence and could exert myself into every room

at once, hear every sound, though I could not determine

its source. Then a cabbie was killed, scooped in our alley,

and a clerk at the corner store disappeared in an aisle mirror.

Thieves had run ladders to the second floor of our house,

then handed down guitars and the dismantled constellations

of drum sets, while the band jammed downstairs.

I'd been seeing the ghost mother of Jeff, a boy

I worked with, every night the last one of her life lived

over and over in what had become my bedroom.

I would watch her frenzied strip routine before she'd

leap out the window, taking most of the fire with her.
With her son, I worked fast food, passing burgers
through holes in safety glass. A co-worker helped me
put it all together, telling me when he drove me home

after work, "That's where Jeff lived up through the fire."
I was often apart from even the girl who for a short while
was enthralled with me, and who drove by the house
one night at 2 a.m. A thief as well, she took too much of me.

As we kissed, she'd close her lashes over my eyes,
blind me to all others in that year of "Killing Me Softly."
The soft rock of that year had turned me soft, too,
leaving me afraid of the dark. When my girl with her friend

drove by to check on me so late that it was morning,
she likely saw me as weak for all the house lights
were lunged on. Outside loitered men with hard bands
of their own, their arms totem poles of watches,

men who had so much time on their hands

that they must have known when I'd roll over in bed

and step up to the glassy pupils we call windows

to watch for everything from threadbare birds

to nippy Ripple bottles being emptied on our lawn.

MY HOMEWORK ATE ME

A true story

Is it fate? A love affair? Or serendipity? Does a house have a soul? Or a heart? Or a need?

In the year 1900, in the city of Minneapolis, past the cow pasture on Eighth Street, a house was built by a Norwegian railroad worker for his family. A duplex, one up, one down, nothing fancy. Big. Sturdy. Warmed by coal. Lit by gas. Interstate 94 runs by there now, but then it was mostly horses.

First time I see it—high ceilings, spacious, light-filled, oak woodwork trimming every window—I'm twenty-five years old and six months pregnant. Three months later, I stand in the first-floor bedroom, naked, sweating, pleasing myself to ease the pain of natural birth. Two midwives kneel on either side, working away like car mechanics. Their long hair sweeps the floor, as behind, my mother, husband, and four sisters sip red wine.

My sister sees my daughter's head emerge, upside-down. With her face still half in me, the child opens her eyes and looks around. *Time to push!* Braced by my husband, I push with all my might. Out slides my daughter. They place her on the pillow. She is blue. She is still. She will not breathe. My daughter remembers this moment. Years later she tells me, *I did not wish to come out. And if I was very still, and very quiet, they might put me back in.* But breathe she must! She takes a breath—turns from blue to purple to red. With the chord still between us, I hold her to my breast. She gives the nipple one lick and latches on. My husband says, *Let's do this again! Right away!*

The marriage doesn't last. The child remains. My daughter dances, sings, and fills the first floor with hearts stacked on hearts, smiling suns, and happy creatures set free of gravity. The child grows lean, a prancing horse. Her hair goes from blond to green to red to black. Her artworks turn from smiling suns to dismembered body parts with bones sticking out and bleeding, winged hearts set free of gravity. She forms a punk rock band, joins the West Bank Hard Times Tall Bike Club, climbs up the homemade bike tall as a young oak, and with her drunken, Black Label, homeless-smelling friends, she rides away.

I am alone. But the second-floor tenants above me are sweet—a nurse and the big, tall man who needs her care. He falls down a lot, BOOM! he falls. And I, below, scrape by on very little, for who needs stuff—with this all this space in which to create? I generate dozens of paintings, plays, and heartbreaks. I trouble-make. I crash my heart against my rib cage.

Twenty years I live here, a single woman, renting the lower duplex. Then the powers-that-be say, *Heidi, this neighborhood needs more stability. You must either move or buy.* Move or buy? I'm just a renter, no homeowner, me. I survive by the skin of my teeth—no patron, no partner, no college degree. But below the earth of this house, my roots have sunk deep. I scrape. I liquidate. I borrow. I buy. Serendipity! Before, the house and I were just pals. Now we are married. Now I may explore its hidden places.

But must not disturb the second-floor tenants—the big, tall man keeps falling up there—BOOM! he falls. One day the sweet nurse tromps out the door—angry at his gift of three hanging flower baskets, now dangling from the porch. She never returns. The flower baskets stay. The man is alone. BOOM! he falls. I'm out of town when they find his body. His testicles, in the summer heat, swollen to the size of basketballs—or hanging flower baskets.

If I'm to keep paying this mortgage, I need a new, living tenant. Up pops one! Old West Banker! Good guy! Friendly. Employed. Enthusiastic. He loves this second floor. Loves it so much he moves his whole family in—grown son, grown daughter, her husband, their baby. He loves it so much, with plastic and caulk, he seals the duplex tight. And with that family up there cooking, breathing, and bathing, over ten years, unbeknownst to me, black mold grows…

Meanwhile, I explore. Up the back stairwell is a padlocked door. In twenty years of living here, this door I've never opened. One night, with a pry bar, a flashlight, and a glass of red wine, I break the padlock. A stairway leads nowhere. On the steep steps are cobwebs, dust, flakes of brown stuff. The opening above plugged with a heavy cube of plywood.

I ascend with my flashlight. In the small space at the top, I squeeze, head braced against wood. *Time to push!* With all my might, the great weight rises. I step into the belly of Noah's ark—Jonah's whale—immense darkness—waiting for me—all these years, one thousand unfinished square feet. I step calf-deep into cellulose insulation. That instant I have a vision—an open space for sharing stories.

The vision is immediate. The dream takes ten years. Sweat, blood, face masks, goggles—one hundred thirty black plastic trash bags filled of cellulose—which I sneak, before sunrise, into various neighborhood dumpsters. My early-rising neighbors think I'm a serial killer.

Meanwhile, the markets crash, my artist income plummets, my day job ends. What to do? I know! I'll move into the unfinished basement and rent the first floor to my daughter and her beau!

The work begins. I tear down old plaster. Free old coal dust. Peel asbestos from old pipes—(I know). Carry 60-pound bags of cement. Put in glass block windows, running inside and out, leveling them—quick! before the mortar sets and before the acid in the mortar eats my hands.

Blue after blue nitrile glove sliced by sandpaper, rusty nails, and blades. Body speckled with primer, paints, and hole filler that in California CAUSES CANCER—but hopefully not in Minnesota. This house that cradled my daughter might take my life—as the hardware store takes all my money.

From within clouds of plaster dust, paint spattered, whilst running up and down the ladder, I hear my neighbor say, *Heidi, you are either really crazy or really industrious.* I nod, *YES! BOTH!*

Tuck-pointing the one hundred-year-old basement, scraping, blowing, wetting, carefully tucking mortar in, not a task to rush, I feel generations of bricklayers working silently beside me. And while finishing the attic, cutting sheetrock at

Menard's, my utility knife jumps. My thumb gushes. I wrap the thumb with masking tape, bungee-cord the sheetrock atop my Ford Escort, drive home, unload in the rain, carry 4-by-4 sheets up three flights, walk to Doctor Steve, get stitched up without Novocain—this is true love.

Every part of this house I have touched and touched again, sanded, painted, scraped, doubling the square footage of livable space.

It's almost done—the attic studio, the basement hideaway—when my daughter's friend says, *This is a perfect place for a sauna.* All work stops while I power-saw, knee-deep in cedar dust, until the house has a sauna.

Meanwhile, unbeknownst to me, the black mold grows. The ideal tenant moves out. My daughter and her beau move up—to the black mold, now visible on the windowsills. In the house I held to shelter her, my daughter sickens. She cannot breathe. The air is oppressive. She wakes in panic, suffocating. I must remove all the radiators, clean behind, see how deep the mold goes, pry off every stick of oak window trim—nine pieces to a window, fourteen windows. Each back side is velvet black with mold.

I build a tiny plastic room. Don mask, goggles, gloves. In summer heat, I pry off each piece, joking (between curses) that this airless little cage is my hot-yoga room.

Carrying the pieces outside, I rush through summer, abating with vinegar, borax, hydrogen peroxide, three times. All round my yard are pieces of my house. I sand, stain, polyurethane, three times. Puzzle all the pieces together. Pound them back in.

With this, air filters, dehumidifiers, and replacement windows, the air on floor two is good. The mold is gone. My daughter can breathe again. So can I. Meanwhile, the back steps crumble, the exterior window rots, the squirrels eat the porch.

My ex-husband returns to help repair. The ex is back there hammering. My daughter and her man are making art and music on the second floor. I'm in the attic writing a new book. The piles of paintings, songs, and performances grow—

And how can I tell you? All these years since I first stepped inside—did I know? That this house would hold me—like a woman holds a lover in her thighs? Or a womb holds a child? Or a casing holds a seed? Does a house have a heart? A soul? Or a need? Is it fate? Love? Serendipity?

I do not wish to leave. And I believe, more than I *own* the house, I *owe* the house. I serve the house. And the house needs me—in this messy, blissful, bloody serendipity.

Fiction
by Vincent Wyckoff

LEMONADE ON A LAKESIDE BENCH

The old man takes a seat on the bench facing the beach. Newly leafed-out branches shade most of the park benches, but this one stands out in the open, allowing late-morning sunshine to warm the wooden seat slats. He closes his eyes and draws a deep breath through his nose. Relaxing into a long exhale, the old man silently recites his address.

Opening his eyes, he looks to the right, north, in the direction of his house, not many blocks away. Then he slowly swings his gaze around to the left, south, in the direction of the coffee shop. He knows perfectly well where his house is, and that it's Sunday and he always reads the Sunday sports section at the coffee shop, but when he looks straight out at the lake again, he shakes his head and mutters an audible sigh of resignation.

"Hmph."

Without a breeze to ripple the surface, the small lake shimmers with a quiet calm in the sunlight. He knows he's been here before, probably many times, but he wonders what the lake is called. Studying the shoreline, he concedes he has no idea where he is. It's as if on the way from point A to point B, someone suddenly placed a park and an eighty-acre lake in his path.

The old man closes his eyes again. He isn't really that old, only recently attaining retirement age, but he knows he looks ten years older than that. A lifetime of heavy blue-collar work has aged him, bent him, enlarging the joints in his aching fingers and stiff knees. The fact that he doesn't know where he is doesn't frighten him. It's happened before, probably dozens of times. His doctor had mentioned dementia, but couldn't predict the arc of the disease.

"This could be as bad as it gets," the doctor had said with a shrug. "A simple, random glitch in your memory." But then he'd slid his stool closer, leaned forward, and lowered his voice. "On the other hand, of course, it could be the beginning of something much worse."

He'd explained how, as the disease progresses, the temporary memory gaps might last longer. The incidents could occur more frequently, perhaps leading to permanent holes in his memory. But at this early stage, the old man still owned a car. He was current on his license and insurance, although the doctor recommended driving as little as possible. "Stay near home," he'd warned, "until we understand how this thing is going to play out. I suggest driving only when necessary, like getting groceries or something." Then he'd looked down, breaking eye contact, as if he knew his words would be meaningless to this tough old man. "Besides, walking most of your errands can only do you good, right? You know, increased blood flow and all that."

The man stares out at the lake while the sun's warmth settles over his head and shoulders. He slouches and tips his head back in an attempt to free his mind and dislodge the memory of his location. From this same bench he knows he's heard the rustle of fallen leaves clattering across the park in the autumn, and felt the sting of icy crystals blown in off the lake pelting his face in the winter. But today, in early summer, while the beach is still too cold for swimming, the playful shouts of children on the playground bounce around the park. Far to his right he looks at the tangled maze of equipment in the playground. Most of the children have removed their jackets and run wild with the enthusiasm of youth.

My home is that way, he thinks, and recites his address once again.

Looking back to the left, in the direction of the coffee shop, he notices a group of several families setting up for a picnic. Folding tables and chairs have been added to the ends of the heavy park tables. Bright floral and checkered tablecloths are held in place with covered casseroles. The families are Hispanic, the old man thinks. Mexican or Guatemalan. Maybe Colombian. The youngest family members race around the tables playing games of chase as the women laugh and chat together while setting out the picnic.

The man smiles and looks back at the lake, off to the west. He tries again to clear his mind, but now he's too aware of his own presence in the park. To others, he thinks, he's probably almost invisible, just another old man sitting on a park bench. A tired old man who isn't as old as he looks. A man who knows his house is nearby; no more than five or six blocks away. A quiet old man on his way to the coffee shop to read the sports section. He isn't upset, not even nervous. He just really wants to remember the name of this lake.

A ball rolls near, breaking his reverie, and stops against his foot. He looks left and spots a young boy cautiously watching him. Standing beside him is a slightly older girl. They both have dark skin, thick black hair, and deep brown eyes. The girl wraps an arm around the boy's shoulders and holds him close. The man wonders if it's done to console or protect.

With the children watching closely, he picks up the ball and spins it in his large hands, causing the black and white markings to blur. As a youngster he'd played football and baseball, hockey and basketball. He didn't know anything about soccer. The boy stepped closer, causing the girl to clutch at him with both hands. But a ball is a ball, the man thinks, and before the children become too agitated, he rolls it to the boy who casually stops it with the side of his foot.

"Good play," the old man says, a chuckle in his eyes.

The boy smiles, his attention never wavering. Moments pass. The man wears a benign grin that the boy appears to accept after serious consideration.

Just as the man is about to resume his contemplation of the lake, the boy kicks the ball back to him. He has to stretch his leg to reach it, but he pulls it to him with his foot, picks it up, and rolls it back to the boy, harder this time. They repeat the play several times, each roll a little faster than the last. The boy is laughing now, and the girl has come closer, intently watching the two play catch.

Then a woman's voice is raised behind them, and the children turn to look. The old man repositions himself on the bench and looks at the woman. She's calling to a man lugging a huge cooler down the hill from the street. The indecipherable words must be Spanish, he thinks, or possibly Portuguese. Whatever it is, the strain in her voice expresses concern, and the old man decides she's probably telling him to be careful. The cooler is massive, one of those designed to be rolled on wheels, but one of them is missing.

The old man surprises himself with how quickly he rises from the bench to stride up the hill. His legs have stiffened after sitting so long, but he pushes through it, swallowing a grimace of discomfort to approach the man and his oversized load. He reaches to help, and the young man flashes him a self-conscious smile, nods, and says, "*Gracias.*"

Moving to one side, the old man wraps thick fingers and swollen knuckles around a handle, realizing immediately that he could easily carry the whole thing by himself. But the young man seems to enjoy the help, smiling and nodding as they walk, muttering chuckling phrases to himself. The difference, the old man acknowledges, is in size. He's probably ten inches taller and fifty pounds heavier than the diminutive Hispanic. Moments later he reaches around, grasps the second handle, and deftly hoists the cooler to an open spot on the table near the women.

The old man steps back when one of the women speaks to him. Now it's his turn to look away in embarrassment. She might just be saying thanks, he thinks, and nods and smiles while looking at his feet. But it seems she's saying much more than that, and it's difficult to stand there with everyone watching. He looks away, at the lake again, thinking it would be even more rude to just walk away while she's talking. Then he spots the girl easing up beside him.

"My mother is offering you lemonade," the girl says and then laughs. "She says she spent all morning squeezing lemons."

The old man looks back at the woman. She smiles, her open-mouthed expression of anticipation much more than the situation would seem to warrant.

"Well, yes," he says, and then quickly adds, "I mean, thank you. *Sí, gracias.*"

The woman's eyes immediately crinkle up with delight, the young man turns away to prepare the charcoal grill, and laughter and chatter return to the park. When the woman offers the paper cup to him, he tries to match her steady grip with his knobby-knuckled fist. The discrepancy reminds him of his youth, when his soft, nimble fingers held his aging grandmother's work-worn hand. She'd squeezed lemonade too, he remembers, but that was decades ago.

The old man nods his thanks again and shuffles back to the bench, careful not to spill. The girl accompanies at his elbow, and he notices that the boy has taken a seat at one end of the bench. As he sits down, it becomes apparent that the girl wants to sit too, so he slides closer to the boy to make room.

He thinks about his grandmother all those years ago on the family farm. He remembers how she squeezed lemons trying to make the tinny-tasting well water more agreeable to the young boy. He smiles when he concedes that her efforts never really worked. But the migrant workers enjoyed it. He'd carry pails of lemonade, covered with heavy cloths to keep them cool, out to the fields where they toiled long days, bent over under the hot sun cultivating soybeans by hand. The migrant farmhands were so appreciative, always greeting him with smiles and laughter. He'd watch as they chatted and joked quietly among themselves, wiping sweat from their brows and adjusting their wide straw hats. He'd never seen skin so dark, hair so shiny black. And they were always much more friendly to him than any of the other adults in his life.

Beside him the boy lightly flips the ball and catches it. He looks up at the old man and says, "My name is Mateo."

At first the old man doesn't know what to think. It's a little startling to go from the farm fields to a park bench so quickly. Finally, he purses his lips, nods acknowledgment, and says, "My name is Howard." And then, for no other reason than force of habit, he once again recites his address.

For a moment all three stare at the lake. It's still a big blank space in his mind. He sips the lemonade and wonders how it can be so much better than the drink from his childhood. Of course, he thinks, it's the water, and suddenly he nods at the shoreline and blurts out, "What lake is that?"

"Lake Hiawatha," the girl says.

"Ah," he replies as understanding and memories tumble back in an instant. How could he forget this place? He closes his eyes and breathes deep through his nose. A pause, and then out loud he recites,

> "To those who love these haunts in nature,
> Who love the sunshine of the meadow,
> And the shadow of the forest,
> To those who love the wind in branches,
> Listen to these wild traditions,
> To this Song of Hiawatha." *

He opens his eyes and gazes out over the calm and silent lake. How is it that I can recite verses of poetry from memory, he wonders, but not recall the name of this lake? I've lived within walking distance of it my whole adult life. He looks first to his left, to the boy, sitting quietly looking out at the water.

To his right, the girl is watching him, and he interprets her expression to mean she wants more. He settles deeper into the bench and drapes an arm along the backrest.

> "Speak in tones so plain and childlike,
> Scarcely can the ear distinguish
> Whether they are sung or spoken,
> Listen to this simple story,
> To this Song of Hiawatha."

Much like the poem, the old man's voice goes soft. He chants the words in metered cadence. The boy nestles in against him, the ball clutched firmly in his lap. The man looks to his right, and the girl is still watching him. She smiles, and so he continues.

> "By the shore of Gitchee Gumee,
> By the shiny big-sea water,
> Stood the wigwam of Nokomis,
> Daughter of the moon, Nokomis."

The old man knew exactly where he was. His house was to the north, not far away. In front of him glistened a lake, a lake whose name he now remembered. And to the south was the coffee shop. As he wrapped his memory around another stanza, he realized he probably wouldn't get to the sports section today, and that was just fine.

* From "The Song of Hiawatha," by Henry Wadsworth Longfellow

HOME

In her eighties

my grandmother wanted to go home

feeling her way along

the walls to get downstairs

coming in her nightgown to clutch me

awake and then out

of my summer vacation bed.

But she didn't know me

who was ten. She didn't recognize her parlor

rocking chair nor the sofa

throw she'd hooked and knotted herself

nor the pungent oilcloth on the kitchen table

as I led her shuffling

in her slippers to the back door.

Instead something nagged at her

something that said

this is not home.

Home is somewhere

else. Perhaps a place she'd been

well or young in

was what she remembered

more vividly now

than this house

she'd lived in for nearly sixty years.

I wondered where it was

she had in mind

if it were real

or a place in the past

still standing in her memory

or who she thought might be there

waiting yet

or if it were just a notion

of what home should be.

It didn't matter.

before we reached the bottom

of the back porch steps

they stopped us.

I never saw my grandmother

lucid again

but always wanting to find that place

she believed she belonged

and I never knew

if she forgave me

that I couldn't take her home.

Heidi Arneson's stories have been called "Visionary—both haunting and hilarious" and "unexpected and glorious." She trail-blazed solo performance with her series of one-woman shows, created spoken word with male inmates, and plumbed small-town secrecy with her gripping first novel, *Interlocking Monsters*. She is a recipient of the Bush Artist Fellowship, Loft/Jerome Minnesota Writer's Grant, and Minnesota State Arts Board Artist Initiative Grant. Her autobiographical workshops have fostered many solo performers. Her plays include *Itchy Tingles*, *BloodyMerryJammyParty*, and *DeGrade School*. Her second novel, *The Chalk Canoe* (Invisible Ink, illustrated by Alberta Mirais), was released in May 2019.

William Cass has had more than 175 short stories accepted for publication in a variety of literary magazines such as *december*, *Briar Cliff Review*, and *Zone 3*. His children's book, *Sam*, is scheduled for release by Upper Hand Press in April 2020. Recently, he was a finalist in short fiction and novella competitions at *Glimmer Train* and *Black Hill Press*, received a couple of Pushcart nominations, and won writing contests at Terrain.org and *The Examined Life Journal*. A former resident of Minnesota, he now lives in San Diego, California.

St Paul writer **Nancy Louise Cook** runs The Witness Project, a series of free community writing workshops designed to enable creative work by underrepresented voices. Nancy is also one of a small number of Solace community artists developing arts programming in conjunction with a transitional housing initiative under the auspices of the Southwest Minnesota Housing Partnership. She spent the first four months of 2019 in Northern Ireland conducting writing workshops with people affected by the sectarian conflict known as "The Troubles." Some of her newest work can be found in *existere*, *The Tangerine*, *Stoneboat*, and *Litbreak*.

Martha Grace Duncan earned a PhD from Columbia University and a law degree from Yale. She is a professor of law at Emory University. Her past writing has employed literature and psychoanalysis to explore such topics as the Amanda Knox case, the metaphor of the criminal as slime, the expectation of remorse in juvenile defendants, and the pleasures of form in criminal law. Her academic publications include a book, *Romantic Outlaws, Beloved Prisons: The Unconscious Meanings of Crime and Punishment* (NYU Press), and articles in the *Columbia Law Review* and the *Harvard Journal of Law and Gender*. Currently, Professor Duncan is working on a book about remorse entitled *Morbid Laughter, Proper Tears*. She is also creating a memoir about her father. Portions of the memoir have been published in the *Gettysburg Review, North Dakota Quarterly, Passages North,* and *Tampa Review*.

Michael Enich is a medical student at Rutgers, The State University of New Jersey Robert Wood Johnson Medical School though he's taking a hiatus from his allopathic medical education to pursue a PhD in social work. Enich is originally from Chicago and graduated from St. Olaf College with a bachelor of arts degree in religion in 2014. Outside of medicine, he rock climbs, sings in his car, drinks too much coffee, and makes his own hummus. What Enich misses most from his days in Minneapolis is watching from the window at Bob's Java Hut as humanity parades and bikes by on Lyndale.

Lisa Fay is a 1978 graduate of Framingham State University with a bachelor of arts degree in liberal studies. She also spent a semester abroad at Digby Stuart College, London, England,

1977–1978. Since then, she has had painting and photography exhibitions. However, poetry is her first love. Ms. Fay has published poetry in magazines, newsletters, newspapers, and anthologies. She has also received two professional development grants from the Massachusetts Cultural Council, two fellowships from the Byrdcliffe Colony in Woodstock, New York, three Walker Grants from the Fine Arts Work Center to take poetry classes, and was selected as a 2004 VSA arts international artist. In addition, she also received second-place poetry honors from the Fensfest Writers' Contest, April 3, 2014. A poem by Fay hung at Boston City Hall from September 2018 to April 2019. On her paternal side, Fay's great-grandmother is a MicMac Indian from Judique, Nova Scotia.

Crystal Spring Gibbins is from the Northwest Angle and Islands in Lake of the Woods, Minnesota/Ontario. She is the editor of *Split Rock Review*, co-editor of *Waters Deep: A Great Lakes Poetry Anthology*, and author of *Now/Here* (Holy Cow! Press), winner of the 2017 Northeastern Minnesota Book Award for poetry. She is a grant recipient from the Minnesota State Arts Board, Arrowhead Regional Arts Council, and Chequamegon Bay Arts Council. Her work appears in *Hayden's Ferry Review*, *Prairie Schooner*, *The Writer's Almanac*, *Verse Daily*, and elsewhere. She lives on the south shore of Lake Superior in northwestern Wisconsin. www.crystalgibbins.com

For more than thirty-five years, celebrated photographer **Wing Young Huie** has captured the complex cultural realities of American society. He has exhibited nationally and internationally—more than half a million people viewed his traveling exhibit in China—but his best known works, *Lake Street USA* and the *University Avenue Project,* were epic public art projects that transformed Twin Cities' thoroughfares into six-mile galleries, reflecting the everyday lives of thousands of its residents. The *StarTribune* named Wing Artist of the Year in 2000, stating, "*Lake Street USA* is likely to stand as a milestone in the history of photography and public art." In 2018 he was honored with the McKnight Distinguished Artist Award. *Chineseness: The Meanings of Identity and the Nature of Belonging* (MHS Press, 2018) is his seventh and most personal book: "I am the youngest of six and the only one in my family not born in China. Instead, I was conceived and oriented in Duluth, Minnesota. So what am I? How does my Chinese-ness collide with my Minnesota-ness and my American-ness? And who gets to define those abstract hyphenated nouns?"

Jayson Iwen has recently been a finalist for the National Poetry Series, the *New Issues Press* Green Rose Award, the *Trio House Press* Louise Bogan Award, the *Periplum* Open Book Competition, the *42 Miles Press* Poetry Award, and a semifinalist for the Brittingham and Felix Pollak Prizes. His published books are *Six Trips in Two Directions* (2006), *A Momentary Jokebook* (2008), and *Gnarly Wounds* (2013). His collaborative translation of Jawdat Fakhreddine's *Lighthouse for the Drowning* was recently released in BOA Editions' Lannan Translation Series, and his edited collection of poems by Jawdat Haydar, *101 Selected Poems*, has been translated into French and republished by Editions Dar An-Nahar. Iwen also serves as the editor-in-chief of the online journal *New Theory* (new-theory.net). He lives and works in the Twin Ports region of northern Minnesota and Wisconsin. jaysoniwen.com

David Jauss was born in Windom, grew up in Montevideo, and attended Southwest Minnesota State University, where he also taught from 1974 until 1977, when he enrolled at the University of Iowa, where he received a PhD in English and creative writing. He is the author of four books of fiction, including two volumes of new and selected stories, *Glossolalia* and *Nice People*; two books of poetry, *Improvising Rivers* and *You Are Not Here*; and the craft book, *On Writing Fiction*. He has also edited three anthologies, including *Strong Measures: Contemporary American Poetry in Traditional Form*, which he co-edited with longtime SMSU professor Philip Dacey. His stories and poems have appeared in numerous magazines and anthologies, and he is the recipient of the AWP Award for Short Fiction (for *Black Maps*), an O. Henry Prize, a Best American Short Stories prize, two Pushcart Prizes, a National Endowment for the Arts fellowship, a James A. Michener/Copernicus Society of America fellowship, and one fellowship from the Minnesota Arts Board and three from the Arkansas Arts Council. A professor emeritus at the University of Arkansas at Little Rock, he teaches in the MFA in Writing Program at Vermont College of Fine Arts.

Jells (Angelica Daniela Bello Ayapantecatl) was born in Zacatelco, Mexico, and raised in south side of Minneapolis. She graduated from Southwest High School, spring 2019, and will be attending Augsburg University with a full ride. She says that she's a "dreamer, daughter of a single CHINGONA mother, first gen., immigrant, native, artist, HUMAN and surrounded by people who I am grateful for. *Estoy aqui por ellos*, I am here because of them. Someone who wishes to take steps forward to make this a world we can actually call 'home' and peacefully enjoy mango ice cream. Seriously, a place where we can all enjoy and share meals together not worrying about our differences in languages, statuses and etc. Art for social justice. That is where my heart lays at and wish to change the world with. *Gracias a todos por lo que han hecho por mi. Les prometo que todo* *su apoyo lo regresare en apoyar a nuestra comunidad y a los demas. Tlazohcamati. Gracias.* Thank you."

Sandra Kacher is a native Minnesotan. Apart from compulsive traveling and a two-year stint teaching in Australia, she has been a happy resident of the Twin Cities. She spent her career as a psychotherapist (which has meant lots of intensive listening), and now that she has retired, she would like to be heard as a poet. Most of her poetry is written at her neighborhood Brueggers, so she is grateful to them for their generosity with their booths. She has been published in *Dime Show Review*, the *Martin Lake Journal* and *We Were So Small*. Home—searching for it, finding it, losing it and belonging to it—are favorite themes, and she is delighted to be a part of this anthology.

Mary Karlsson grew up in Forest Lake and now lives in Hastings. She has a background in business and public administration and currently has a business consulting practice. Although she has been writing for the business world for many years, this is her first piece of creative writing submitted for publication. She is married to Kent, and they have two grown sons who live in Minneapolis. www.marykarlsson.com

Kristin Laurel has been employed as a nurse for thirty years. A great deal of her writing examines trauma and the complexities of human experience. She owes her passion for poetry to the Loft Literary Center in Minneapolis where she completed a two-year apprenticeship. Her work can be seen in *CALYX*, *Chautauqua, Gravel, Portland Review,* and *The Raleigh Review,* among others, and her poetry has been featured on NPR. She is the author of *Giving Them All Away* (Evening Street Press), and *Questions About the Ride* (Main Street Rag Publishing).

Enrique Lucas is a jiu jitsu practitioner, music composer, and occasional writer. Enrique has loved fiction since before he could pronounce "Darth Vader," as well as any good story about the chronic condition of human suffering. After living in an RV for almost a year and blogging about his travels, he decided that writing was for people who didn't want to live in reality.

Mbeke Waseme is a writer who was born in the UK to Jamaican parents. Her first poetry book, *Exploring all of me* was first published in 1987 and was republished in 2019. She is the author of *Make the Changes, Feel the Joy*, and *How to Work and Live Abroad Successfully*. She has chapters in *This is Us: Black, British and Female* (2019), *Trusted Black Girl, Challenging Perceptions and Maximizing the Potential of Black Women in the UK Workplace*, edited by Roianne Nedd (2018). Her body of work also includes a series of articles and interviews on health and business, which first appeared in the UK publications *African Business and Culture*, and *The Alarm* magazine. She currently writes for *Diversity Business* and *Turning Point* (UK). Her short stories and poems are in *Fifth Estate*, *Dovetails*, *Pure Slush*, and *The Writers Caféuse press*, and her essays and academic articles have been published in *Pambazuka* and *72M*. Mbeke is currently living in the UK and working on an anthology of writing by women who have lived and worked abroad. Mbeke has traveled to Minnesota and says, "I really enjoyed the diversity of the Twin Cities. Unfortunately, I did not enjoy the snow as I generally dislike anywhere which is colder than The UK!"
www.mbekewaseme.com

Teresa Ortiz is a writer, poet, and spoken-word artist, as well as a mother and educator. As an immigrant from Mexico in Minnesota, her writing aims to describe her identity, the land where she has lived, and the lives that have touched her own.

Teresa is a member of Palabristas, a Latino spoken-word collective. Her poems have appeared in several chapbooks, and she has performed and read poetry in different outlets throughout the Twin Cities. She authored a book of testimonials of indigenous women, *Never Again a World Without Us: Voices of Maya Women in Chiapas, Mexico* (EPICA, 2001). One of her short stories, "El Rio" was included in the collective *Lake Street Stories*, published in 2018.

Deborah Schmedemann is four years into the second phase of her adult life. After teaching thousands of law students and writing legal textbooks, she now volunteers with immigrants and writes personal essays. Her work has been published in topical anthologies on themes such as change and joy, and she compiled the book, *Thorns and Roses: Lawyers Tell Their Pro Bono Stories*, her project for the Master Track Program in Creative Nonfiction at the Loft Literary Center in Minneapolis. She delights in nurturing the three grandchildren of her two daughters. She lives as close as one can get to the Mississippi River in south Minneapolis and now counts Chicago as her second city, thanks to those grandchildren. She travels internationally with her husband, Craig Bower, and around the block with her dog, Columbo.

Grace T. Andreoff Smith is Yup'ik from Pitkas Point, Alaska. Grace is a boarding school survivor. She has lived in Minnesota since 1959. She is the mother of seven wonderful children and grandmother of 11. Grace enjoys acting with New Native Theatre, playing bingo, spending time with her children and watching her grandchildren in their sporting activities. Grace is the former Princess of the Four Winds for the Saint Paul Winter Carnival senior royalty.

Alicia Smith is Yupik from Pitkas Point Village in Alaska. Alicia works for the State of Minnesota. Alicia has a bachelor's degree from the University of Minnesota-Morris and a master's degree in tribal administration and governance from the University of Minnesota—Duluth. When not working at DHS, Alicia and her mom enjoy acting with New Native Theatre, running, golfing, and spending time with her family.

Bart Sutter is the only writer to win the Minnesota Book Award in three different categories: poetry, fiction, and creative non-fiction. His most recent collection is *Nordic Accordion: Poems in a Scandinavian Mood*, published by Nodin Press in 2018. He has written for public radio, he has had four verse plays produced, and he often performs as one half of The Sutter Brothers, a poetry-and-music duo. He lives in Duluth and has read his poems throughout Minnesota, from Hallock to Austin, from Grand Marais to Luverne. www.bartonsutter.com

Thom Tammaro has lived and worked at the western edge of Minnesota for thirty-six years in Moorhead. He recently coedited, with Alan Davis, *Visiting Bob: Poems Inspired by the Life and Work of Bob Dylan* (2018). He is the recipient of three Minnesota Book Awards, as well as fellowships in poetry from the Minnesota State Arts Board, the Jerome Foundation, and the Loft-McKnight Foundation. *23 Poems* was published by Red Dragonfly Press in 2016.

William Torphy's short stories have appeared in *The Fictional Café, ImageOutWrite* Volumes 5 & 6, *Main Street Rag, Miracle Monocle, Sun Star Review, Burningword Literary Review, Bryant Literary Review,* and *Chelsea Station*. He works as an art curator in the San Francisco area.

The poet laureate of Grand Rapids, Michigan, from 2007 to 2010, **Rodney Torreson** is the author of four books of poetry.

A fifth book, *The Jukebox Was the Jury of Their Love*, is forthcoming from Finishing Line Press. It is a full-length collection of poems pertaining to rock music, with poems about the Beatles, the Rolling Stones, Bob Dylan, Janis Joplin, Joni Mitchell, Leonard Cohen, Van Morrison, Lucinda Williams, and many other recording artists. In addition, Torreson has new work scheduled to appear in *Artful Dodge, Canary, Miramar, Poet Lore, Seems*, and *Tar River Poetry*. Torreson says his poem was written about living in the Selby/Dale area during 1972, while attending Concordia College in St. Paul, where he was a student from 1969 to 1973, then again during the 1975–1976 academic year.

Susan Terris' recent books are *Familiar Tense* (Marsh Hawk, 2019); *Take Two: Film Studies* (Omnidawn, 2017); *Memos* (Omnidawn, 2015); and *Ghost of Yesterday: New & Selected Poems* (Marsh Hawk, 2012). She's the author of six books of poetry, sixteen chapbooks, three artist's books, and one play. Journals include *The Southern Review, Georgia Review*, and *Ploughshares*. A poem of hers appeared in Pushcart Prize XXXI. A poem from *Memos* was in *Best American Poetry 2015*. Terris is editor emerita of *Spillway Magazine* and a poetry editor at *Pedestal*. Terris says, "I spend every summer in Park Rapids, Minnesota, where I own a family lake house (we call it a cabin, of course) that's been in my family almost one hundred years."
www.susanterris.com

Sarah Brown Weitzman, a past National Endowment for the Arts Fellow in Poetry and Pushcart Prize nominee, is widely published in hundreds of journals and anthologies, including *New Ohio Review, North American Review, The Bellingham Review, Rattle, Mid-American Review, Poet Lore, Miramar,* and *Spillway*. Her latest chapbook, *AMOROTICA*, is forthcoming from Darkhouse Press.

Born and raised in Minneapolis, **Vincent Wyckoff** dedicated a career to the U.S. Postal Service. His first book, *Beware of Cat, and Other Encounters of a Letter Carrier*, celebrates the stories of people on his route. Prior to that, he attended the University of Minnesota and served a tour of duty in the U.S. Army. For a short time, he lived on the north shore of Lake Superior, from which he developed the background for *Black Otter Bay*, his first work of fiction. Mr. Wyckoff and his wife, Sybil, are longtime residents of south Minneapolis. They have three children and six grandchildren.

Raised in a nomadic upbringing, **Ahmed Ismail Yusuf** is the author of three books: *Gorgorkii Yimi,* a collection of short stories in Somali, *The Lion's Binding Oath*, a collection of short stories in English, and *Somalis in Minnesota*. His play *A Crack in the Sky* was produced at the History Theatre in Saint Paul, and others were performed at Pangea as well as Mixed Blood Theatre. He has a bachelor of science degree in creative writing and psychology from Trinity College in Hartford, Connecticut, and an MPA (Master of Public Affairs) from the Humphrey Institute of Public Affairs of the University of Minnesota.

First poetry editor of two pioneer feminist magazines, *Aphra* and *Ms.*, **Yvonne** has received several awards including NEAs for poetry (1974, 1984) and a Leeway (2003) for fiction (as Yvonne Chism-Peace). Recent print publications with her poems include *Bryant Literary Review, Pinyon, Nassau Review 2019, Bosque Press* #8, *Foreign Literary Journal* #1, *Quiet Diamonds* 2018 (Orchard Street), and *161 One-Minute Monologues from Literature* (Smith and Kraus). She is the author of an epic trilogy: *Iwilla Soil, Iwilla Scourge, Iwilla Rise* (Chameleon Productions). Excerpts from her verse memoir can be found online at AMP,

Tiny Seed Literary Journal, Poets Reading the News, Rigorous, Headway Quarterly, Collateral, the WAIF Project, Brain Mill Press's Voices, Cahoodaloodaling, Edify Fiction, and *American Journal of Poetry*. More excerpts are forthcoming in *Ragweed, Colere,* and *Beautiful Cadaver Project Pittsburgh.*

William E Burleson is the publisher of Flexible Press, Minneapolis, Minnesota. Burleson's short stories have appeared in numerous literary journals and anthologies to date, including *The New Guard* and *American Fiction* 14 and 16. Recent work includes editing and publishing *Lake Street Stories,* a short-story collection featuring his and the work of eleven other Twin Cities' authors that came out in September 2018, and his book of three short stories, *Tales of Block E,* published in 2017. He is now working on a novel, *Ahnwee Days,* the story of a small town that has seen better days and the mayor who tries to save it. Previous to writing fiction, he had published extensively in nonfiction, most notably his book, *Bi America* (Haworth Press, 2005). For examples of past work and more information, visit www.williamburleson.com.

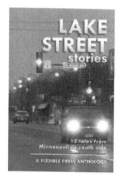

Made in the USA
Middletown, DE
09 June 2021

41646491R00144